W9-ARQ-532

Rachel Vail's
The Friendship Ring Series

what are friends for?

AN APPLE PAPERBACK / SCHOLASTIC INC.

New York • Toronto • London • Auckland • Sydney
Mexico City • New Delhi • Hong Kong

No part of this publication may be reproduced in whole or in part, or stored in a retrieval system or transmitted in any form, or by any means, electronic, mechanical, photocopying, recording, or otherwise, without written permission of the publisher. For information regarding permission, write to Scholastic Inc., Attention: Permissions Dept., 555 Broadway, New York, NY 10012.

ISBN 0-590-37454-0

Copyright © 1999 by Rachel Vail.
All rights reserved. Published by Scholastic Inc.

APPLE PAPERBACKS, SCHOLASTIC and associated logos are trademarks and/or registered trademarks of Scholastic Inc.

12 11 10 9 8 7 6 5 4 3 2 1   9/9 0 1 2 3 4/0
                                                              40
Printed in the U.S.A.
First Scholastic printing, October 1999

what
are
friends
for?

Look for more books in

The Friendship Ring Series:

to

Arlene and Arthur,

whose generosity, energy,

and love are inspirational

what
are
friends
for?

one

Some growth spurt. My mother says an inch, but I know she was tilting the book. I know it was only half an inch, maybe three quarters. She wants to reassure me, but the only time I ever think about how short I am is when everybody keeps consoling me that height doesn't matter and that anyway I'll have my growth spurt soon, when my adolescence starts.

I'm not worried about the fact that I still care about current events and my schoolwork either. I know most other seventh-grade girls have only two interests: popularity and boys. That stuff bores me, honestly; when those conversations come up — *Do you think he likes me? Are you mad at me?* — I go over my times tables in my head and wait for a more interesting topic. I know that makes me seem behind the other girls in my grade, less mature, less normal. I can't help it. It's not that I'm antisocial; I'm actually very friendly. It's just that I can't help noticing that the seventh-grade girls who used to be reasonably intelligent people have recently become idiotic, single-minded bimbos, one after another, as the hormones hit. People like CJ Hurley, a gifted ballerina and a sensitive friend, lose all perspective and every interest when some dirty-fingernailed but popular boy calls her up on the phone.

I wonder when it will happen to me.

two

This morning when I got to school, I had only a few paragraphs to go in the chapter I was reading, so I stumbled up onto the curb with the book still in front of my face. When I finished the chapter, closed my book, and looked up, Morgan Miller was staring right at me. I looked behind me to be sure it wasn't somebody else, but no, it was me.

I don't waste my time keeping up to the minute on who is in and out, but everybody in our grade knows that Morgan is always at the center of things. She tends to be very angry at somebody at least once a week and to have intense opinions about what is and isn't acceptable — clothes, behavior, all the details of life. I care a lot about moral issues like free speech and homeless people, but not so much about what an acquaintance wears. Morgan scares me a little.

So when she stared at me like that, I said something like, "You coming into school?" We've always been friendly, though distantly, and she looked particularly fierce right then. I don't care who likes me or doesn't, but it's not good to be the one Morgan is angry at.

She sprinted over to me, latched onto my arm, and dragged me by the elbow into school, whispering, "Some people think they are so great." She stormed off to her own homeroom when I asked her who.

In homeroom, permission slips for next week's seventh-grade apple-picking trip were handed out. Zoe Grandon, who sits next to me, opened her big blue eyes wide and smiled at me. I guess she was excited about the trip, which I was dreading because last year, as everybody in Boggs Middle School knows, two seventh-grade couples got caught kissing behind a haystack on the apple-picking trip. For weeks after they came back all the boys in the whole school were talking about it, pretending to cough, but really saying "hay-stacking" and meaning *kissing*. It's what made me dislike boys last year, all that talk of *hay-stacking*, *hay-stacking*, like all they thought girls were good for, all of us who've been their buddies and first basemen and lab partners, all they thought of when they saw us, was *hay-stacking*. My brother, Dex, told me I needed to relax. He thought it was funny four of his friends got suspended. I thought the whole thing was insulting and annoying. But that's just my opinion.

All through the announcements, Zoe fiddled with a silver ring on her finger. When the bell rang and Zoe and I were walking out of the room, I complimented her on the ring.

"Thanks," she said with a huge smile. "I got it this weekend." She held her hand out for me to get a better look.

"Pretty," I said. "I like the knot."

Zoe nodded. "It's a friendship ring. CJ has the same one."

"Oh," I said. "That's nice." CJ Hurley's mother and mine are very tight; we go on family vacations together, but CJ and I aren't especially close. She is nervous and timid, and not too interested in anything but ballet, which is her life. She's very talented. Ballet and, lately, boys. And always Morgan. As far as I knew, CJ's best friend was Morgan, not Zoe.

Zoe was adjusting the ring on her finger as we got to the door of her French classroom. I decided it was none of my business who got friendship rings with whom. Zoe asked me, "Did you have fun putting together the project for English class over the weekend?"

"Fun?"

"It was harder than it seemed, I thought."

"I agree," I said. The assignment was to fill a brown paper bag with ten objects that, taken together, would give a complete picture of who you are. I'd worked all weekend on it and felt pretty confident about the ten things I'd chosen. "I can't wait to present it," I told Zoe.

CJ approached us, rubbing her right hip. I asked her if it was hurting.

She shook her head very quickly and said, "Um, a little. But, I mean, no."

"That's good," I told her as encouragingly as I could. She always seems to be in the midst of an anxiety attack.

"Thanks," she said, clasping her hands tightly behind her back. Tommy Levit walked past us. He's the boy CJ had decided she liked last week. CJ covered her face with her hands. I resisted groaning.

CJ lifted her face and announced, "Tommy asked me out."

"Oh," I said. "When?"

"Friday," CJ said.

"Congratulations." I had no more to say about that

subject. I don't know what everybody sees in Tommy Levit. He's a twin, with Jonas Levit, which is inherently interesting, I guess. And he is nice-looking in a generic American way, with dimples and a sarcastic look on his face, but I really don't see why so many of the girls in our grade act stupid around him, especially after last year, when Morgan went out with him and he kissed her so hard and so unexpectedly that she dumped him and hasn't really spoken to him much since. He's the kind of boy who likes to tease — and CJ is someone who can't easily withstand teasing. But since it wasn't my business, I didn't say a thing. I opened a folder holder and put away my permission slip.

I noticed CJ watching me, and realized she wouldn't be able to go, because of dance. No wonder she seemed even more tense than usual. "So you can't go on the trip, huh?" I asked her.

"What?" Zoe asked. "Why?"

Morgan, who was passing us on her way to Spanish, said, "Dance."

"Hey, wait up," CJ called to her, and chased her down the hall. She is often chasing after Morgan, apologizing or complimenting. Now Zoe chased after CJ, asking, "What is Olivia talking about, you can't go apple picking?"

CJ shook her head, trying still to catch up to Morgan. I slowed down. I hate how desperate my friends seem lately, how nervous.

"Why can't you go?" Zoe wasn't getting much response from CJ, so she turned and asked me, "Why can't CJ go apple picking?"

"We don't get back until six-thirty," I explained, since I had caught up.

"Yeah? So?"

"So," said Morgan, stopping outside Spanish. CJ almost bumped into her. "CJ has dance at four on Mondays. Not that she even likes ballet anymore, but . . ."

That surprised me. "You don't?" I asked CJ.

"It's complicated," CJ answered, nervously fingering her hair. She is so pale, you can see the veins on the side of her forehead.

"You like it or you don't," Morgan told her, with disgust in her voice. "How complicated is that?"

"You can't miss one day?" Zoe asked CJ.

CJ shook her head. "Something could happen, some casting director could come to watch. You can't. And especially, my mother?"

Morgan blew her long, dark bangs out of her eyes. "CJ's mother says, 'It's important to devote yourself to something so you'll stand out from the crowd.'" She mimicked CJ's mother perfectly. I've heard her mother say those exact words, in fact.

"Really?" Zoe asked. "She says that?"

"All the time," Morgan answered. "Makes me feel great."

"She doesn't mean anything against you," CJ apologized. In fact, CJ's mother thinks Morgan is a bad influence on CJ, coming from a messed-up family with an immature father who ran off to California with a young floozy and a nasty angry mother with no manners. CJ's mother and mine talk every day. They both wish CJ would be best friends with me instead. CJ's hands fluttered up to her hair again. "She just, it's true that . . . I really wanted to go apple picking."

Zoe's smile tightened. "Or at least hay-stacking."

"Yuck," I said. It slipped out.

"I like apples," CJ protested in her whispery voice.

"Yeah, apples." Zoe turned the ring around on her finger. "An apple a day." The bell rang. Zoe gasped. She's the only one of us who takes French instead of Spanish. She ran back down the hall toward her class.

Morgan grabbed my elbow again and asked, "Don't you think it's pathetic when all some girls obsess about is boys, boys, boys?"

I glanced at CJ, who turned away. I didn't want to insult her, but the truth is, I do think boy-craziness is pathetic and gross. I nodded at Morgan. She yanked me into Spanish class with her.

After Spanish, Morgan pulled my arm down the

corridor. The rest of me followed. Morgan whispered, "CJ thinks she's above everybody else. Doesn't she?"

I asked what she meant. CJ is a family friend; we protect each other even if we don't always enjoy each other's company.

"CJ is even more impressed with herself than usual, don't you think?"

"I hadn't noticed," I whispered back.

Morgan nodded. "Yeah, you're right. It is hard to tell, since she's always Miss Prima Ballerina. You're absolutely right."

That wasn't exactly what I had meant. I held the cafeteria door open, and Morgan dragged me through it. She walks so fast it was a challenge for me to keep up with my elbow.

"But now that Tommy Levit asked her out . . ." Morgan sighed, shaking her head. I sat down and she squeezed in beside me, at the end of the table. Morgan cupped her hand over my ear and whispered, "And did you see her ugly ring?"

"The friendship ring?" I asked.

"Yeah, hard to miss, the way they're waving their hands around, huh?" Morgan kicked off her sandals and folded her foot underneath her. "Guess CJ is pretty thrilled with herself, getting to be best friends with Zoe the Grand One."

That was witty of Morgan to come up with, I thought; nobody had ever called Zoe Grandon *the Grand One* before. I opened my 7UP and repeated, "Zoe the Grand One."

"Yeah." Morgan took one of my pretzel sticks, waved it around in a small circle beside her head, and whispered, "Hooray for them and screw us."

I laughed and the 7UP I'd just sipped went right up my nose. "Ouch," I said, which made Morgan laugh so much she had tears in her eyes. I offered her more pretzels. She was sitting so close to me I could feel the warmth from her arm on mine. I usually like more personal space than that, so I finished up lunch quickly and suggested we go outside for the rest of the period.

She said, "Absolutely."

That's another thing about Morgan — she's very emphatic. When the bell rang, she got hold of my elbow again, and we walked that way to our lockers and then to English/social studies. People watched us pass.

three

I felt something.

It's hard to tell if it was what you're supposed to feel, because of course I've never felt anything before, anything like it. I've had strep throat about twenty times, so as soon as it starts to come, even before the throat culture can be positive, I know if I have it or if it's just swollen glands; on the other hand, when I got chicken pox last year, I had no idea what was happening to me. I thought maybe it was adolescence or the flu, until I got itchy. So, since I've never had a crush before, there is no way of telling if that's what just happened to me. Maybe it's a virus, for all I know. Or mumps. Although I think I got inoculated against that.

But I definitely felt something.

Lou Hochstetter was giving his oral report to the class, and I was trying to pay attention even though I already know about as much as I care to know about World War Two armaments from Lou Hochstetter's last fifteen oral reports on the subject. I've been in Lou's class since kindergarten; I could probably do a report on World War Two weapons myself, with very little time in the library.

Today was the first time a teacher didn't seem terrifically impressed with Lou. He really is very impressive. He was on PBS when he was eight, his tanks and guns all lined up as he explained them and the host smiling the way beautiful but nonintellectual adults grin at kids who are smart. Like, *Isn't he cute?* but also, at the same time, like, *We're all in on the joke that this kid is way too bright ever to be cool and beautiful like me.* Lou's overenthusiastic mother, who is running for mayor now, brought a video of the PBS show into school the next week. We had an assembly. The whole school sat in the dark, elbow-wrestling one another over the armrests, half watching the video of Lou with all his little World War Two scale models and the host with all her big teeth. When the lights came on, the principal called Lou up onto the stage of the auditorium, and Lou took a bow, one hand on his belly and the other behind his back, his elbow sticking up behind him as if he had a terrible backache. Most people clapped for him, especially the teachers and his mother.

But today, although his armaments were all on display again across Mrs. Shepard's desk, there was no bowing. He finished his presentation and looked up, smiling and expectant, at Mrs. Shepard, but she just stood there. Lou smiled bigger, his braces showing way back to the ones on his molars.

I looked over at Mrs. Shepard, to see what was going on. Mrs. Shepard is known as the best teacher in Boggs Middle School, tough but brilliant. At first glance, you might think she looks like a kindly old grandmother from a fairy tale, little and white-haired, slightly hunched forward, but once you see her eyes, you stop thinking that. They are bloodshot and squinty, with big black pupils and pale blue irises. I can't look at her and talk at the same time, and I am not at all shy. Somebody like CJ, who has trouble talking anyway, shrivels up any time Mrs. Shepard comes near.

But Lou Hochstetter is the biggest boy in seventh grade. Of course, size does not determine courage; I consider myself relatively brave and I'm the shortest girl in the grade, four foot nine inches unless you believe my mother, in which case, four foot nine-and-a-half. Still, Lou has been on TV.

Mrs. Shepard pointed her tongue at her upper lip. After a full minute, she said, "And?"

"And?" Lou asked back, still smiling. I noticed his gums were red and swollen, all puffed up. His neck was breaking out in purple blotches, and a bead of sweat was rolling down his forehead. It paused on his eyebrow.

"And what does this panoply of World War Two armaments reveal about Louis Hochstetter?" Mrs. Shepard asked him.

The sweat ball dove from Lou's eyebrow into his left eye. "What do you mean?" he asked her, blinking furiously. I sit right up front, so I had a perfect view of the battle between the sweat ball and Lou's eye.

Mrs. Shepard, unaware, said, "The assignment, Mr. Hochstetter."

I reached into my desk to find him a tissue. Lou, still half smiling, placed his hand carefully beside the Lee Enfield gun on Mrs. Shepard's desk.

I pulled a tissue out of the small traveler's size box I keep in my desk in case of emergencies, but it didn't seem like quite the appropriate time to get out of my seat, barge up to the front of the classroom, and say, *Here, you have sweat in your eye — want a tissue?*

Lou leaned more and more of his weight onto his hand, until he was diagonal. The rest of us sat perfectly still and waited.

"The purpose of the assignment was to reveal yourself in all your various aspects," Mrs. Shepard said finally. "Have you done that, Mr. Hochstetter?"

"I, sort of . . ." Lou's voice squeaked, so the "sort" was a very high note, and the "of" was rumbling low. I crumpled the tissue by accident.

"Oh?" asked Mrs. Shepard.

Lou's bare hand wiped his forehead, where a battalion of sweat balls had mustered. "I'm interested in," he started, then swallowed. His lips didn't quite meet, over the braces. He swallowed again, and then, turning pale, said, "Interested in World War Two. Armaments."

Mrs. Shepard's voice came over my shoulder at Lou as she asked, "And is that interest all there is to Louis Hochstetter?"

Lou swallowed hard and answered, "Pretty much."

Mrs. Shepard said, "Hmm."

Lou blinked his eyes twice and then surveyed his ten choices of World War Two scale models. They looked like toys, as if he had brought out ten Matchbox cars or ten Beanie Babies. As he'd been pulling them out, one by one, I had felt outdone. My presentation, which I had worked on all weekend, seemed so trivial in comparison to his that I'd been insulting myself for being too superficial and flighty a person, watching him pull these bronze-cast pieces so confidently from his Sack. He had mastery over some bit of world history while I had soccer ball earrings and a charcoal pencil. I felt like a trivial person as I watched him.

But his field of expertise ended up being just a set of toys. I have to admit I felt a little bit better about myself. At least I did the assignment right, I thought; at least there's more to me than one narrow interest. I'm not proud of having thoughts like that but sometimes I do, it's awful but I do.

Lou stood at Mrs. Shepard's desk for a few seconds, looking at his things, and then instead of just dumping them into the brown paper bag, or sweeping them in as I would've done at that point — anything to get away faster — he gently picked up the 2.3 mortar, turned it over in his palm to inspect it, and wrapped it carefully in its bubble wrap before lowering it softly into the bag.

That's when I felt it, this thing I am wondering if maybe it is how the first pang of a crush feels.

My insides got hot and my skin felt chilled. My first thought was, *Fever.* Then I thought, *Wait a sec, maybe not*. My hands rubbed the tissue as I watched Lou rewrap his scale models and painstakingly place them, one by one, back into his bag — not dropping them, but lowering them all the way in, taking all the time necessary to do it right — while everybody in the class waited and watched. It seemed extraordinary to me, after what Mrs. Shepard had just said — like he was oblivious to the fact that she had just stripped his artillery pieces of their value. Or like he disagreed. It seemed so radical, what he was doing. I wanted to see Mrs. Shepard's reaction, but I couldn't stop watching Lou take care of his things.

Then, as Lou walked past me going back to his seat, I felt what I can only describe as some kind of force field, or magnetic energy, or maybe static electricity. The whole thing may just be a matter of an over-heated classroom in September causing some static electricity exchanges, when oppositely charged people pass too near each other. The whole thing is very likely to be scientifically explainable, a matter of laundry products not used.

Or else, I'd just entered adolescence. Emotionally, anyway. My body remains concave.

four

ommy Levit began his report and CJ sat up straighter. Like me, Tommy had ten reasonable, varied, appropriate objects in his bag — a plastic dinosaur, a Red Sox ticket, a photograph of his family at the beach. Not like Lou's. When Tommy finished, Morgan, who sits behind me and in front of Lou, passed me a note:

Sorry I'm such a moody mess. Tommy thinks he's so great. Ha! I have to tell you something URGENT. Your best friend, Morgan.

It surprised me enough to distract me from my new possible situation with Lou. *Your best friend, Mor-*

gan? If I had to choose who was closest of my friends, Morgan would not have made the shortlist. Until today, in fact, Morgan barely tolerated me. If I'd thought about it at all, which I didn't really, I would've said we were distant friends or acquaintances at most. I missed whatever happened between her and CJ, I guess — a fight or something, maybe over Tommy, and it must've happened over the weekend. Sometimes I feel out of sync with what's going on.

My best friend?

"Cornelia Jane Hurley," Mrs. Shepard called.

I knew better than to look at her, poor CJ. I kept my eyes on my desk and willed her the strength to get up there and do her report. Nothing happened, nobody moved. I reread Morgan's note and wondered what *URGENT* thing Morgan might have to tell me, and hoped it wouldn't be more nasty things about poor boy-crazy, tongue-tied CJ.

CJ still hadn't budged. I quickly wrote back to Morgan, *Want to come over after school today?* and flipped the note back to her.

Finally, CJ passed me, walking slowly, but of course gracefully, toward the front of the class. It was clear she was terrified. I don't know what it is that scares CJ so much about talking in public. It's ironic because she performs in ballets in front of hundreds, but getting up in front of nineteen kids she's known her whole life is torture.

While CJ presented the contents of her bag — basically one ballet prop after another — I imagined what I would do with Morgan after school.

My best friend.

We have a pool table, but Morgan can't play and I think doesn't like to. We have plenty of board games, but it seems to me that it is suddenly not the thing anymore to play games. Over the summer, everybody grew out of being a kid, everybody except me, and now they're no longer interested in anything but bodies and boys. My brother is a year older than I am, so I've always watched what he does to see what I'd be doing the next year — like I knew in second grade that I'd get to play violin in third grade, and then that year I found out I'd start team sports the year after — but Dex is still playing board games with his friends, and sports, and pool; not talking about the opposite sex all the time, at least that I've heard, and not saying all the time, *I'm so ugly,* or *I'm so stupid,* or, my least favorite, *Who do you like?*

It's not that I want desperately to be popular or anything. In fact I usually prefer to be alone, but I know that it's important to have friends and for the past week I've been feeling very clumsy in that way. I was actually planning to go to the library after school and try to find a book on seventh-grade girls.

I could tell Morgan I like Lou. She's very big on the *Who do you like* question, and until now, I've always just said, *I don't like any of the boys much at all*, because I don't, or didn't. I always tell the truth, it's a vow I've made to myself. If Morgan asks me that question today, though, I'll have to answer that I might actually like Lou Hochstetter. For the first time, I can see how that's an interesting question to turn over and over in your mind. *Do I like him? Does he like me?* I could spend some time on that. *What if he likes me, too?* Lou Hochstetter and Olivia Pogostin. They sound good together, actually.

Those thoughts made me jittery. CJ finished her presentation, which was very boring, but Zoe the Grand One (I have nothing against her; I just like that) applauded. People looked back at her, surprised.

As Zoe applauded, I wondered again what the UR-GENT thing was that Morgan wanted to tell me, and then, I realized — Morgan likes Lou, too.

Of course. She did pass me the note after Lou's presentation. Obviously his vulnerability up there with his World War Two paraphernalia had touched Morgan just as it had touched me. How could I not have realized? It was so obvious. My heart was thumping.

As CJ took her seat, I turned to look at Morgan.

Morgan's head was ducked down almost to her desk. Lou sits behind her, and since Lou is very tall, I saw his face instead. We made eye contact. He tilted his head a little to the side, so his shaggy brown hair swung down into his eyes. I smiled a little. He began to smile, too, and the silver of his braces peeked out from between his lips. I blinked, then glanced at Morgan.

Caught.

Morgan's eyes had tears in them. Obviously she'd seen me staring at Lou, smiling at him, flirting, if I'm honest. That's what I was doing, I have to admit; I was flirting. A flirty girl. That's who I'd suddenly become, of all things, exactly the opposite of how I'd always thought of myself, exactly what I've always sworn I'd never be. Nobody ever wanted me for a best friend before. Morgan suddenly did, which was odd enough, and then practically confided that she liked Lou — now here I was, betraying her already.

Morgan stood up abruptly, banging her knees into her desk, which tilted forward onto my chair. I caught it before it fell over and dumped her stuff. She was clutching her crumpled Sack and asking Mrs. Shepard if she could go to the bathroom. Before Mrs. Shepard could finish reminding her to leave her Bring Yourself in a Sack project, Morgan was out the door, her Sack still in her fist.

"Zoe Grandon, you're next," Mrs. Shepard said, but I raised my hand before Zoe had a chance to stand up.

"Yes, Olivia?" Mrs. Shepard asked me.

"May I go to the bathroom, too?" I asked.

"When Morgan returns," she answered, and turned to raise one eyebrow at Zoe, who was clattering around at her desk.

"I wanted to, um, see if Morgan needs help," I said in as confident a voice as I could manage.

"Doe she have an injury?"

I thought about it. *An injury?* "Not exactly," I answered.

"Well, then."

I sunk low in my seat as Zoe walked toward the front. I closed my eyes. Five minutes into adolescence and I'd already fallen in love, gotten a best friend, betrayed her, and lost her. If things continue at this pace, I'll be dead by tomorrow.

five

At the end of Zoe's very funny and creative presentation, Morgan returned to class. Her eyes were red and her jaw was clenched, but she stood straight and crossed the room with those long steps she always uses. I tried to catch her eye, but she wouldn't look at me.

When Morgan's name was called next, to give her report, she dropped the note on my desk as she passed. She had written, under my invitation to come over after school, *Yes*. I was so surprised I had to reread it a number of times. It kept saying Yes, and I kept being surprised.

Morgan's stuff was different from mine and most people's — instead of souvenirs from vacations or tokens of her interests, Morgan's Sack was full of her personality: a box of red-hots represented her sweet tooth; one of her baby teeth was there to symbolize the babyish parts of herself, parts that she's done with. The last item was the best, in my opinion. It was the bag itself, once it was emptied, as a representation of the parts of herself that she hasn't yet created.

I turned quickly to look at Mrs. Shepard. She looked blown away. She even complimented Morgan.

I never realized Morgan was so deep.

We didn't talk after class or on the way to gym, and she didn't drag me by the elbow, which I realized I had already gotten used to. We were in different groups for gym, so after school at the lockers was the first time we were pretty much forced to deal with each other since the Lou thing.

"You ready?" Morgan asked, slamming her locker shut.

"I walk home," I said, unsure if she already knew that.

"I have my bike," she said, starting to walk toward the front entrance of school. "I'll ride you."

As I was hurrying to catch up with Morgan, Lou Hochstetter slammed into her. He'd been running toward the front door from the band room with his trombone case held in front of him like a shield.

"Oof," he said, tripping but continuing toward the door.

"Watch where you're going!" Morgan grumbled. She turned around to me, shaking her head and smiling a little. I smiled back. She slowed down, and when I caught up with her, she whispered, "His presentation today, didn't that kill you?"

I nodded. We nodded together, holding each other's eyes, and Morgan covered her heart with one hand, the way CJ and her mother do sometimes. She leaned even closer to me, until her forehead tapped mine.

"Ouch," I said, and she said *ouch* at the same exact time. Then I lifted my hand to rub the spot that had clonked against her, although it didn't actually hurt, and she was doing the same exact thing. We smiled at each other and started laughing.

"What's so funny?" Roxanne Luse asked, angrily, from across the lobby.

I was about to assure Roxanne that we weren't laughing at her, when Morgan said, "Nothing," and grabbed me by the elbow to drag me outside.

"Your face is funny," Roxanne called after us, which made both Morgan and me laugh. Morgan used to laugh that way with CJ, bending over each other, in on the same joke that nobody else in the room picked up.

I'm not usually much of a laugher, but I was practically choking, doubled over there in front of school.

When Morgan gasped, "Do you think she meant my face or your face?" a snort came out of my nose, which knocked Morgan over onto her knees, and I fell down laughing right beside her.

"You OK?" asked my brother, Dex, who was suddenly standing above me. When I looked up into his concerned face, it convulsed me with hysterical laughs all over again. Morgan, too. Dex just stood there, waiting for us to collect ourselves. Dex is used to girls falling all over themselves giggling in front of him; he's learned to be patient about it.

Dex is very good-looking. We don't talk about it much because physical appearance is not what matters, my parents both say, but I know people can't help staring at my brother. One time this past summer, when we were waiting in line for the movies, a woman in pink pants and a hair scarf was staring and staring at us, which we ignored — we're multiracial and Boggs is very white, so sometimes ignorant people are rude — until she finally met up with us at the refreshment counter and said to my mother, "Your son is stunning."

My mother smiled slightly and answered, "I have two beautiful children."

"Of course, of course," the lady said, shuffling away with her box of Dots gripped tightly in her meaty hand.

It's not the first time something like that has happened. Dex has big brown eyes with thick, long eyelashes, a small, straight nose just like my mother's, curvy brownish lips like my dad's, and a slow smile that shows mostly his bottom teeth. He's on the tall side, with broad shoulders and narrow hips, and he wears his hair really short. His skin, like mine, is the color of tea with milk, a combination of Mom's half-Filipina khaki and Dad's half-African-American brown. I know I'm not repulsive-looking — I'm sort of cute, actually — but my looks aren't especially remarkable except maybe for being small for my age, and light brown. People stare at Dex.

As Morgan and I sat there on the pavement catching our breath, Dex asked, "Where's your other half, Morgan?"

"It's Monday," I reminded him. "CJ has dance." Dex always makes fun of CJ when we go away, our two families — *Where's your other half, CJ?*

"She always has dance," Morgan added. "We barely see her. So I don't know what you mean, other half."

"No offense intended," Dex said. "Sorry."

"Can we go?" Dex's friend Andrew asked him.

"Yeah," Dex said, but instead of leaving asked me, "How was the Sack project, Oblivia?"

"Fine," I said. That's what he calls me, Oblivia. He thinks I'm oblivious to social situations, just because I'd rather read than hang out.

"Did Shep like the soccer ball earrings?" Dex asked me. He'd helped me plan the Bring Yourself in a Sack project over the weekend and let me practice presenting it a few times to him. I'm his favorite person in the world, he always tells people. The soccer ball earrings were his idea.

"I guess so," I said. He's the only one who calls Mrs. Shepard Shep. I noticed Morgan tilting her head when he said that. "Morgan's was really good," I told Dex.

Morgan pulled her knees in to her chest and said, "Mine was stupid."

"No, it wasn't," I said.

She glared at me, then ducked her head down to her knees and looked up at Dex through her bangs.

"How stupid?" Dex asked her.

"Totally embarrassing. I hate stuff like that, being on display."

"I know it," Dex said, poking the crew-cut, muscular boy next to him. "Last year, Travis brought ten pictures of himself. Shep tore him apart for it."

"Don't remind me," groaned Travis.

Morgan nodded. "That's like Lou Hochstetter. Shep ate him for lunch."

"The kid whose mother is running for mayor?" asked the other boy with Dex, a skinny blond-haired guy named Andrew. "My mother is working on the campaign," Andrew explained, kicking a stone.

"Yeah," Morgan mumbled. "His project was really boring. Ten World War Two toys."

Andrew smiled. "I remember him. Wasn't he on TV or something?"

"It wasn't boring," I said. My voice sounded a little screechy. I retied my sneaker, thinking maybe I should sign up to work on Lou's mother's campaign, too. When I looked up, Dex and his two friends were grinning at each other, raising their eyebrows. "What?"

"Sounds like love!" Travis taunted. His mother died three years ago, so now he lives with his father and two older brothers and one younger sister, who wears about twenty barrettes all over her hair every day. Dex says you have to make allowances for Travis because with what he's been through, anybody might get in fistfights. I feel bad for him but still he's obnoxious. He was making kissy faces at me, saying "Lou and Olivia sittin' in a tree, k-i-s-s-i-n-g."

"Shut up, Travis," I said, standing up and dusting myself off.

"Don't be ashamed," Travis taunted.

"I'm not," I told him, my voice shaking just when I needed and expected it to sound strong and certain.

Andrew pushed his glasses higher on his nose and said, "If you like him . . ."

"If I liked him, I'd say so," I interrupted. "I just said his project was good. What I meant by that was, his project was good."

"Mmm-hmm," Travis said knowingly. "First comes love . . ."

Dex caught Travis in a headlock and told him, "You don't know my sister. If Oblivia liked a boy, she'd march right over and ask him out. Trust me, she would. Right, Oblivia?"

They all looked at me. Dex smiled so proudly I had to say, "Absolutely."

Morgan stood up and jammed her fists into her hips. "Olivia would never like Lou Hochstetter. He's a total geek."

I couldn't look up at Dex or his buddies. I put my hands on my hips, too, hoping I'd look as sturdy as Morgan. I wanted to stand up to her and defend Lou, and point out that I knew she liked him, too — but I also didn't feel like dealing with Travis's teasing. That's probably why Morgan had said that, not so much out of nastiness or dishonesty. It was none of anyone's business who we liked, anyway.

"But if you liked him," Dex prodded. "You'd admit it, right? And ask him out?"

"Obviously," I said. My voice cracked, like Lou's.

"Sure you would," mumbled Andrew. "No way, Dex. It's what I was saying — girls have it so easy."

"Yeah, right," Morgan grunted, blowing at her bangs.

"No, boys do the asking out," Andrew mumbled. "So nobody says no to you."

"What century do you live in?" I asked him.

"Go easy," Dex told me, putting his arm around Andrew. "Andrew got rejected today."

"Did not!" Andrew punched Dex in the stomach. "She likes me too much as a friend, that's all!"

Dex danced backward, laughing. "OK! OK! Down, boy!"

The three boys scuffled away. Dex waved to me and yelled that he'd see me when he got home from Andrew's later. I waved back. Morgan was looking down at her toes.

"Your presentation today really was good," I told her.

"Right," she said. "Mrs. Shepard was really impressed when I dumped that box of red-hots all over the floor." She picked up her black backpack and shimmied into it.

"No, I think she really liked the way you did it," I insisted.

"Not that I care what Mrs. Shepard thinks," Morgan grunted. "But thanks. At least it wasn't as bad as Lou Hochstetter's, huh?"

I looked her straight in the eyes and forced myself to ask, "You like him, don't you?"

"Lou Hochstetter?" Morgan asked.

"You can tell me." I picked up my backpack by the middle loop and watched it hanging from my fingers. "I wasn't really flirting," I lied.

I hate lies. I think lying is cowardly and a bad habit, an easy way out. I felt angry at myself for doing it. "Actually . . ." I corrected myself. "OK, maybe there was flirting, but I'm not in love with him."

Morgan started laughing. Soon she had to lean on her bike, she was laughing so hard, and it tipped over into the other five bikes still locked to the rack. They all crashed over, which had Morgan down laughing on the pavement again. I stood there holding my backpack, looking around at nothing, waiting.

"I thought you were serious," she finally gasped.

I didn't know what to say.

She laughed again and said, "I never knew you were so funny, Olivia."

"I'm not," I said.

"Like *that*," Morgan said. "You act so straight, everybody thinks you're just boring and smart, but you're really way more sarcastic than I am, aren't you?"

I shrugged. "I'm actually just boring and smart, I think."

"Right," she said, nodding. "Subtle. Lou Hochstetter. I'm so stupid."

I raised one eyebrow. I learned to do it this past summer. It's a useful response, sometimes, when you can't think of what to say.

"You kill me," Morgan said. "You're way funnier than CJ."

"CJ?" CJ is about as serious as a person can be. I never thought of myself as particularly funny, but funnier than CJ Hurley is not a colossal achievement.

Morgan blew from the corner of her mouth up at her long bangs. "I used to be best friends with CJ."

"I know," I said. "I sort of thought you still were."

"Yeah, but over the summer we really grew apart." Morgan stood up again and adjusted her black polo shirt.

I twisted the strap of my backpack around my finger. "How come?"

"I don't know. I guess she, I just can't stand it when people are so obsessed with boys they can't think of anything else," Morgan insisted. "That's how you are, too, I know."

"Obsessed with boys?" I started picking up all the bicycles so I wouldn't have to face her. I'd been rational and nonobsessed until fifth period.

"Right." Morgan chuckled. "You and I are so alike," she said. "We both hate all the boys and all conceited people, and we're both sarcastic."

"Hmmm," I said, noncommittal.

"And we both hate flirty girls. Right? That's what I like about you — you aren't embarrassed to be an egghead. Don't tell anybody, but I like math, too, like you said today it was your favorite subject? I used to pretend I didn't get it, but I do. I could learn a lot from you. You're so confident. And sarcastic."

A Good Humor truck bell rang, out on Oakbrook Road. I was relieved, ready to change the subject. I pointed toward the truck and yelled, "Hey! Ice cream!" I love ice cream. Whenever Dex and I see the Good Humor truck, we always yell, "Hey! Ice cream!"

"You don't still like Good Humor, do you?" Morgan asked.

I watched the truck roll past. "It's my favorite food," I said.

She cocked her head toward me. "You! Just like the Lou Hochstetter thing! You got me again! I'm used to CJ, how straight she is. I have to get used to your jokes. Lou Hochstetter. Can you believe your brother's friend thought you'd like Lou? The biggest geek in our class?"

I should've said, *I actually do like him.* But I wasn't sure — it was a new feeling and maybe it really was static electricity. And here was Morgan Miller, the most powerful girl in the whole grade, acting like I'm in on secrets with her. Not that she was acting like Lou being a loser was a secret — actually, she made it sound like an accepted fact. I closed my mouth over my crooked teeth and didn't argue, as weak as that is. *Don't let her intimidate you,* I coached myself.

"Not that we like any of them, but, please . . ." Morgan sighed, then picked up my book bag and latched it into the rattrap of her bicycle. "OK. You sit on the seat, and I'll ride you. Just keep your feet out of the spokes."

Morgan's helmet was dangling from her handlebar, and mine was back in my garage. It's very dangerous to go two on a bike. My mother trusts me not to do stupid things like that. I stood beside Morgan's black-and-orange bicycle, not saying or doing anything as she unlocked it from the rack.

"What's wrong?" Morgan asked, tightening her own backpack straps.

"Boy's frame," I remarked casually. "My bike is a boy's frame, too." *Stay true to yourself, Olivia! Be strong!*

"I'd never ride a girl's," she agreed, tilting the bicycle toward me. "Here, I'll hold it steady for you."

"I can just walk," I offered.

"You scared?"

"It's not safe," I said. There, I'd said it. It's important to be true to yourself, my parents always say, and they're proud of me that I don't follow the crowd. Dex leads the crowd. I do my own thing, and if the crowd is doing it, too, fine; if not, fine, too. Morgan had just said she could learn about being confident from me, in fact. I rested my hands on my hips. Confidently. I hoped.

Morgan stood with her legs wide apart, holding her bike balanced in her two hands. She looked at me so blankly, I wasn't sure if she was angry or hadn't heard me or was weighing her options or just thinking about something else.

"Morgan?" I asked.

"Fine. You can have the helmet," she offered, unbuckling it from the handlebar.

"No," I said. "That's not the point."

"Or we can skip it."

"Why don't we just take turns walking it?" I asked her.

Her lower jaw slid forward.

"What?" I asked.

She turned away from me and rebuckled her helmet onto the handlebar. "Forget it," she said, and tore my backpack out of her rattrap. "If you don't want . . . Forget it."

She lifted her right leg over the back of the bike as it was already moving and rode fast away from me, without her helmet on. I stood there next to my backpack and watched her ride off, wondering what in the world had happened.

six

I walked home alone. I like be-
ing alone. I walk home alone most days; it's my time
for myself, when I can imagine things like, *What if I
could fly.* Sometimes I sing show tunes in my head or
even out loud, if I want. I love show tunes; I memo-
rize entire shows off the CDs, then sing all the parts.
Sometimes I imagine being a Broadway actress, per-
forming on opening night with the lights reflecting in
my eyes, but usually when I'm singing the songs, I just
imagine that the heartbreaking or exciting thing the
character is experiencing is actually happening to me.

As I got to Oakbrook Playground, where I used to
play, I was being John Adams in the play *1776*, frus-
trated and fed up with the dillydallying of the Conti-

nental Congress. I was practically marching, I was feeling so zealous and patriotic and angry, having to do all the work of creating this country practically single-handedly. "Does anybody see what I see?" I sang louder than I meant to.

"What do you see?" a meek voice asked me.

Without thinking, and since the question was right in rhythm with the song, I sang, "I see fireworks!"

Then I stopped myself, which is good because it is a very dramatic part of the song (if I'd continued I would've been belting "I see the pageant and pomp and parades!"), and poor Lou Hochstetter was sitting on a swing in Oakbrook Playground, looking at me like I'd lost my mind.

"You see fireworks?" he asked. "Really?"

"It's a song," I said.

"I know. *1776*." Lou stared down at his feet, which I noticed for the first time were very long and so narrow that the shoelaces were pulled tight enough to make the two sides meet, no tongue showing. The bows ended up huge loops.

I felt myself blushing. "I can't believe you know *1776*."

Lou's head snapped up, and he glared at me angrily. "I actually do know about more than just World War Two."

"I know," I said. "Sorry."

Lou pulled at his lower lip.

"I thought your project was very good."

"Shut up," he mumbled. "You don't have to mock me. Everybody else already did."

"I wasn't," I said. "I really thought it was good. I wouldn't say so if I didn't. Honestly."

"Give it a break." His voice cracked again so the "break" came out soprano. He kicked the sand under the swing.

"Who mocked you?"

He shrugged one shoulder.

"All the boys?"

He wrapped his arms around the swing chains, hung his head, and nodded a little.

"Do you care?"

"Everybody teased me. 'All there is to you is World War Two.' Gideon, Tommy, even Jonas, everybody. Of course I care."

"But they're wrong," I told him.

"They're my friends."

"Some friends." I sat down on the last swing, so there was one between us. We just sat there on the swings for a while, not talking, not really swinging, either, just sitting. Together. I almost said, *Well, boys are nasty,* but my mother says you shouldn't generalize like that or it's prejudice and besides, Lou is a boy, so how would that make him feel? Not better. I thought about telling him that I'd be getting braces at the end of the week and asking him how it felt, or if he had any advice, but I didn't really need any advice. I considered bringing up the apple-picking trip, but Lou had been one of the boys who spent months pretending to be coughing but actually saying hay-stacking, and meaning *kissing*. I wouldn't want him to think I was hinting that I wanted to kiss him or something.

I cleared my throat. Lou glanced over at me, but when I didn't come up with any words, he went back to studying his long, skinny feet. I traced circles with my toes in the sand. I could volunteer to campaign for his mother, but that seemed really pushy. I could mention that Morgan had signed a note to me *Your best friend,* but I wasn't sure where to go with that. I wasn't even sure what to think of it. I didn't even know Morgan's middle name, and though of course I knew her birthday, since we've been in each other's class since pre-k, I don't know her favorite color or her thoughts about God. And she doesn't know mine either, so how could she call me her best friend?

Well, that didn't seem exactly right as a topic to bring up with Lou either, so I started to swing. I pumped my legs and pumped some more, higher and higher, up to the level where there was a pause on the top ends of the front and back trajectories. When I peeked out of the corner of my eye, I saw Lou swinging high next to me. I smiled at him and he smiled back.

I started dragging my feet to slow down, and realized I was thinking, *I shouldn't be swinging here with him — we're too old for this and besides, he's a total geek.* I planted the toe of my sneaker hard into the dirt, angry at myself. I should never let myself be swayed by someone else's shallow judgments of a person. I was surprised and angry with myself. I gripped the swing chain and asked Lou, "Do you want to go out with me?"

Lou dragged his shoes to slow down. "What did you say?"

I closed my eyes. "You heard me." Did he honestly expect me to repeat it? I'm strong, but there are limits.

"Did you say, 'a *garoudabee*'?" Lou asked.

"What? Why would I say *garoudabee*?"

"I don't know," Lou answered.

I was furious. "*Garoudabee?*" I hate being mocked. At least the girl Dex's friend Andrew asked out had the tact to make an excuse if she didn't want to go out with him. I hate boys, I decided. Forget adolescence, forget strength in resisting peer pressure; I wanted to go home. "Why don't you just . . ."

"Just what?" Lou asked.

I got off my swing and picked up my backpack. Without turning back to him, I said, "If you don't want to, why don't you just say no?" I started walking away, muttering.

"I don't even know what a *garoudabee* is!" Lou yelled. "I never had a *garoudabee*. OK? Satisfied?"

"*Garoudabee?* That's not even a word."

"So why did you say it to me? You said, 'Do you want a *garoudabee!*'"

"No!" I yelled back, stomping over to yell right in his face. "I said, 'Do you want to GO OUT WITH ME.' You big . . . stupid."

"Oh."

"Obviously."

"How should I know?" Lou mumbled. "You have a really good vocabulary. Lots of times you say words I don't know."

"Thank you," I said. I started walking toward home again.

"No, wait," Lou said. I heard the chain clink as he got up off the swing. "Did you really say that? Ask that?"

"Forget it," I said again, walking faster. I heard his footsteps behind me.

"What?" he asked. "I didn't hear what you said."

I turned around and found myself looking right at his armpit. "I said, 'Forget it!'"

"Oh," he said. "I don't have such great hearing. Sorry."

"That's OK," I said.

"It's been a, sort of a rough day for me. Everybody's been yelling at me, all day."

"Sorry," I told him again.

"I can't."

"Can't what?"

His face turned red and he looked down at his sneakers. "Can't, you know, *garoudabee.*"

"That's OK. Never mind." *It's been a rough day for me, too,* I thought.

"Not that I don't want to. I do. I would. I mean, that would be, phew, um, fine, great. But I'm not allowed to date until I'm sixteen."

"Oh," I said. "OK." I turned to leave again. I've never wanted to get home so bad in my life.

He walked next to me. The waist of his jeans was about up to my chest, so to talk he hunched over and ducked his head. "At least I think. That's the rule for my sister, so I gotta figure. My mother is a feminist, so, I gotta figure."

I walked faster, but his legs are twice the length of mine, so he kept up.

"But I, if I could, then, I mean, when I'm sixteen,

I'll, well, I guess that's a long time away, but, you're allowed?"

I closed my eyes and kept walking. "Forget it."

"This was a terrible, terrible day for me until now."

We'd reached Hazelnut Road. "'Bye," I said, sprinting across it.

"Your project was really good, too!" he yelled after me. "Sorry about . . . you know."

"Don't mention it." *Please.*

I ran the rest of the way home.

seven

At night, after dinner, we take our things to the dining room table and all get our work done. Mom turns on some music, always classical, usually Vivaldi or Mozart, then gives herself half an hour to read a novel before she starts grading her students' philosophy essays or working on her own. Dad opens up his laptop and begins sorting through his stack of medical journals. Dex takes the longest getting settled, usually going to the bathroom or to get a drink of water as soon as he sits down, then opening and closing textbooks for a few minutes, trying to choose which homework to think about first. I like to do my homework in the order of my day — first Spanish, then math, science, English, and social studies — it keeps things neat.

When our grandparents are over, which happens more often now that Papa retired and Nana gets sick of having to deal with him alone, they sit at the dining room table, too. Nana does the crossword puzzle. Papa just sits, his pale bluish-gray eyes roving over each of us. It makes Dex crazy.

"Why can't he sit still?" Papa asked Mom. Papa never talks directly to anybody.

"Leave him alone, Dad," Mom answered without looking up from her book.

"You shouldn't let him chew his pencil," Papa commented, and then burped. Loud. "Pardon me," he said.

I knew better than to look up at my brother, whom I could hear snickering. I told myself I was being disrespectful, and curled my foot under me.

"Doesn't she have slippers?" Papa asked about me.

Mom didn't answer, so I didn't say anything, either. After a minute, Mom asked, "Olivia — what are you working on?"

"Spanish vocab."

"Need help?"

"No, it's easy."

"Dex? How about you?"

"Actually," Dex said mischievously. *Oh, no,* I thought. "Actually, I'm filling out this application for all-county chorus?"

"Yes," Mom said. We all looked cautiously at Dex. It didn't sound like something he'd be having trouble with.

"And I have to say what race I am. So what am I?"

Papa burped again and said, "Pardon me."

"Black," Nana said without looking up from her crossword puzzle.

"But that leaves out three quarters of my heritage," Dex said. "That leaves out you and Papa, completely. And Grandma Beth, too. I never even really knew Grandpa Joe."

"I'm black," said Dad.

"You're half black," I told him.

"I'm working," he muttered, going back to typing.

"When people look at me, they see an Oriental," Nana said.

In unison, Mom, Dex, and I said, "Asian American."

"You can say all you want, all of you, that you're mixed race," Nana said. "You can list your ethnicities and percentages, but when people look at you they see a black. And if you call yourself anything else, people will think you're ashamed."

"I'm not ashamed," I told her pretty calmly, considering. "Why does everybody keep accusing me of that? I'm just uninterested."

"What do you mean?" Mom asked, laying her novel on the table.

"I mean, it doesn't matter anymore, race. Not to-day, at least not to me or my friends or any intelligent, moral person." I slammed my Spanish book shut, for emphasis.

Nana said, "You'll learn."

"I don't want to learn that," I told her.

Nana said, "You'll learn anyway."

Without looking up, Dad said, "They won't learn anything if they don't do their homework."

"Do you think Nana is right?" I asked Dad.

"Factually?" he asked. "Or morally?"

"Well, I think she's wrong on both counts," I said, controlling my anger. "I don't think everybody sees two black kids when they look at me and Dex. I know not everybody does, because I don't, for one. That's not what I see when I look at us, or anybody. I don't see black or white."

Mom asked, "What do you see?"

I see fireworks! I thought, but I managed to say in-stead, "I see a person. A whole, a particular person, not part of a group."

"Good," said Mom, glaring at her mother. "I'm proud of you."

"So what should I check off?" Dex asked.

"Leave it blank," I suggested.

Dex chewed on his pencil. "Other?"

"Yes," Dad answered. "Now, shh."

"Other," Dex mumbled. "That's us, Obliv. Our group. Other."

"Well, that's not how I think of myself." I opened my textbook again and had gotten about halfway through my Spanish vocab words when Dex flung a rubber band at me. I looked up. He was grinning. "We should have a secret handshake," he whispered.

Mom was engrossed in her novel again, her knees bent against the edge of the table and her back curled deep in the chair, with Papa staring at her. Nana was erasing an answer, and Dad's fingers were flicking at the keys. I signaled Dex to be quiet and went back to vocab.

Dad stood up abruptly and went to the kitchen to get the phone. He paced back into the dining room, waiting for an answer, and muttered, "I'm just really worried about this guy — young guy, fifty-four, no history, came in with a massive right hemisphere stroke and we gave him TPA and he didn't bleed, at least right away, but — Hello? Yes, it's Dr. Pogostin calling." He walked into the hallway, still talking. Mom shrugged at me and Dex. None of us really understands what Dad is talking about, when he talks neurology to us.

"Olivia likes Lou Hochstetter," Dex announced.

Mom, Nana, and I lifted our heads and stared at Dex, then at each other.

"Irma Hochstetter's son?" Mom asked.

"He's white," Dex stage-whispered to Nana, who shrugged elaborately, picked up her crossword puzzle, and headed for the family room, grumbling about the uncomfortable dining room chairs and lack of peace.

"I don't like him." I told Mom. *Not anymore.*

"Travis thinks she does," Dex insisted. "But that she just won't admit it."

"I like him as a friend."

"Travis says she's ashamed."

"Travis is an idiot," Papa said. I smiled at him. He stood up, straightened his slacks, and ambled toward the family room after Nana. He can't stand being away from her for more than a minute. I think it's very romantic. Nana thinks it's very annoying.

"Why would you be ashamed?" Mom asked me, leaning forward across the table, her shiny braid plunking from her shoulder down onto her folders.

"I wouldn't be," I said, and bent over my Spanish textbook.

"Because he's a geek," Dex whispered loudly.

"Why is he a geek?" Mom asked. Nobody answered. "Why?" she asked again.

Finally I said, "He just is, Mom."

"Well, what's geeky about him?"

"Everything," Dex said. "The way he walks — *de-doe, de-doe.* He's still obsessed with World War Two guns. He comes to school with bed-head. He plays trombone."

"I happen to like trombone music," I said, then shook my head and tried to concentrate on my homework.

"Hmmm." Dex leaned back in his chair. "Maybe Travis is right."

I slammed my hand down on my notebook and said, "We're *friends!*"

"Geeky guys are the ones to go for," Mom said.

"To *go for?*" Dex asked her. "To *go for?* How cool are you?"

"Hey," Mom said. "Pretty cool."

"You think so?" I asked her hopefully. "I mean, about geeky guys?"

She lowered her glasses and focused on me. "Something going on with you and Lou Hochstetter?"

"No," I said quickly, feeling myself blush. "Nothing."

"Touchy, touchy," Dex said.

"You know I don't like anybody, Mom. I mean, *that way.* I just meant . . . Forget it."

Mom raised one eyebrow, the way she'd taught me to do. I doodled in my notebook. She always knows my thoughts.

"Geeks are smarter," Mom said slowly. "More interesting."

"Blech," I said.

"Oh, Olivia, don't be like that." Mom curled herself back into place, deep in her chair. "I went through a cool dude phase, myself. Thank goodness I grew out of it."

Dad paced by, still on the phone, saying, "Intracranial hemorrhage."

"Way out of it," Dex told Mom.

Mom opened her mouth wide. "What is that supposed to mean?

"Dad is not exactly cool dude material."

Dex and I grinned at each other. My father wears his pants too high and keeps pens in his shirt pocket, and wears thick glasses and white socks. He's very smart, scientifically, and very kind, but he's nobody's idea of cool.

"Well, thank goodness he's not," Mom said as Dad wandered silently back into the room, distractedly holding the phone by its thick antenna.

"Why?" I asked.

Mom smiled. "Sometimes the charmers are the real jerks. Right?"

"Hmm?" asked Dad. "I'm sorry. He's crashing. They might have to do a hemicraniectomy. I'm just, sorry, what did you need?"

"Nothing," Mom told him.

"I'm sorry," Dad said, kissing Mom on the top of her head. "I'm just thinking if we . . . No, because the risks . . . I just wish there were a right answer. You do nothing, he's gonna die, or maybe not, maybe he just gets better. Or you give him the TPA, and maybe he bleeds into the stroke and instead of healing him, I'm making him worse. Or, it might save his life. I just . . . There's no way to know which."

Dad stood there leaning on my mother's chair, shaking his head and staring into the middle distance.

The phone rang. It was still in Dad's hand so he was startled. He fumbled with the buttons, found POWER, and barked, "Dr. Pogostin."

Then he squinted at me, as if trying to place where he'd seen me before.

"Yes, she's here. May I tell her who's calling? Hold, please." He held out the phone to me and said, "Lou Hochstetter?"

I grabbed the phone from his hand. "Hello?" The mouthpiece smelled like Dad, spicy and warm.

"Olivia?" I heard Lou's creaky voice in my ear.

"Yes." Dex and Mom were staring at me. I stood up and walked out into the hall.

"Do you have a partner for the math project yet?" Lou asked. "I was thinking, for the, remember today, what Ms. Cress said? Choose a partner, for doing the

Maya number system? In math today. We have to make up our own number code? I was wondering if you'd want to be partners. With me, I mean."

"Sure." The only thing a boy would ask me is to do math. Morgan was right in the first place, I'm boring and smart. *That's good though,* I told myself. *I wouldn't want to be any other way.* I wandered into the front hall bathroom and stared at myself in the mirror.

"Great," Lou was saying. "We'll make up a really complicated code. Nobody will crack it. This'll be great."

"Great," I echoed. I looked boring and smart to myself, with my same braids and big eyes I've always had. I'd been thinking lately I had nice eyelashes, sexy even, because they're thick and curled, but maybe not. Which is fine. All that is just surfaces, which I am not interested in. Not at all.

"Let's each start working on it tonight," Lou was saying. "And we can show each other our ideas tomorrow. OK?"

"OK," I said. I turned away from the mirror and went back into the hall. *Better get back to homework,* I was thinking. *That's what's important.*

"That's not why I called," Lou said.

"It isn't?" I stopped walking.

"No," he said softly. "It was, I was, I wanted to say,

thank you. About what you asked me earlier. In the playground. If you remember. If you don't, that's OK. You might've, um, forgotten, or, but I . . ."

"No," I whispered. "I remember."

"So, um, about that, um, issue, I just wanted to say that even though I can't, you know, officially, I, just wanted to say that, I've noticed you."

"You what?" I sunk down on the floor, hugging my knees.

"What I mean is, I, if I could, if I were allowed, you would be the girl I would most want, to, um, could we just, um, what I wanted to ask you is . . ."

I waited, smiling.

"Could we just, you know, *like* each other? That's probably stupid. You probably think that's stupid."

"No," I said.

"OK," he said quickly. "That's what I thought. OK. Forget it."

"No," I told him. "I meant, yes. Sure. That's fine."

"Yes?" Lou asked. "That's great. Wow. That's so great. OK. Wow. Really?"

I smiled. "Yeah. Sure."

"So, great," he said. "Wow. Phew. I took a shower before I called you. To be, um, clean. Anyway, oh, I didn't mean to tell you that. Forget I said that. Anyway, you can hang up because you're probably, like, getting ready for bed, or, I mean, you don't have to tell me what you're doing."

"Homework," I said.

"Right," said Lou. "Figures. You're so smart, too. Wow. But, so, go ahead, see you tomorrow, thank you, I'm hanging up now, 'bye." He hung up.

I laughed and hung up, too. I just sat there in the hall a minute.

When I finally ventured back into the dining room, Mom and Dex both looked up at me expectantly. I stood the phone beside Dad and sat down resolutely in front of my homework.

"So, how's Lou?" Dex asked.

"We're friends!" I said. "Doesn't anybody but me and Dad have any work to do?"

Dad tore his eyes away from his laptop screen and asked me, "Who's Lou?"

"A friend," I said, trying to stop smiling. "Just a friend."

eight

The next morning, Morgan grabbed me when I was halfway out of the backseat of Mom's car and dragged me by the elbow past Zoe and CJ into school, whispering as if nothing had happened between us at the bike rack, the day before. "Did you bring in your permission slip?" she asked me. "What should we get for the bus ride?"

"I'm not sure," I said, stopping myself from asking if we were sitting together next Monday on the bus to apple picking. I'd been half expecting her to give me the Silent Treatment.

"We'll figure it out," she whispered, toying with the lock dangling from my locker. "Right?"

"Right." Last week we were just acquaintances. I

wasn't at all sure how to act toward her. I closed my locker and she fastened the lock for me.

"I'll pick you up after homeroom," she whispered.

"I, OK," I agreed. *I really could just meet you at Spanish, like usual,* I almost said, but she's free to take an extra long walk if she feels like it, I told myself. I don't know how she managed it, but by the time Zoe and I emerged from our homeroom, Morgan was already there, waiting for me. She dragged me by the elbow toward Spanish. Zoe was left standing there alone. During class she passed me a note that said, *Hola, amiga.* I didn't pass one back, but I did smile at her. She waited by my desk after the bell rang.

On the way to math, Lou walked with us and said, "Wait till you see what I thought of."

Morgan turned her back to him and whispered to me, "What does *he* want?"

I cupped my hand over her ear and whispered through her silky hair, "He's my partner for the math project."

"I sort of thought . . ." she mumbled. "Never mind."

I didn't know what to say. *Does being best friends mean you're automatically partners for everything?* I didn't mean to do the wrong thing. I was just unclear about the rules.

The bell rang as I was slipping into my seat. When we split up to work with partners, I pulled my chair to Lou's desk, but I turned away from him and looked toward Morgan, who was slumped over Roxanne Luse's messy desk. Morgan looked at me blankly, maybe angrily. I flared my nostrils at her. She cracked up, which made me feel terrific. Nobody ever thought I was funny before.

"Hi," Lou said.

"Hi." I tried to think of anything other than, *He likes me.* "So, a code . . ."

"A code." We made eye contact. I quickly looked down at my paper. With my peripheral vision, I saw his face turning purple. I think mine was, too. I glanced over at Morgan, who smiled at me. It felt like my birthday or something, like I was the one in the tiara and the chair with the Mylar balloon.

I thought of a million questions I wanted to ask Lou, none of which had to do with numbers. For example, I thought of asking why his family had a rule about whether you can go out with somebody and at what age, but I guess my family is different from most. I can't imagine my parents making that kind of rule, or that they'd think it was any of their business; even if they did tease me about Lou's phone call, they certainly didn't press me for details or tell me what I could or couldn't do. That would've been so rude. It may be one reason Dex and I get along so well with our parents: They respect our privacy and our ability to make responsible decisions. If I'd ridden with Morgan on her bike, for example, it's not that my mother would punish me or ground me like other mothers might, but just that she'd be surprised and disappointed in my poor judgment. I think. I don't know because I would never betray her trust.

The bell rang incredibly soon, and Morgan yanked me away. I barely said 'bye to Lou. Morgan whispered, "Let's get out of here!"

All day long it was like that: Morgan putting her back to everybody and whispering only to me, and Lou blushing every time he looked my way.

At the end of soccer practice, Lou jogged over from the other field where the boys had had their practice and headed straight for me with his big, doofy grin. Dex, who is the starting center on the boys' team, was waving at me, too, his cleats knotted at the laces and draped over his shoulder. I waved back and Lou, thinking I was waving at him, yelled, "Hi!" Dex tilted his head and pointed his thumb at Lou, then sped up to overtake him.

Morgan wedged herself between me and them and whispered, "Walk me to my bike?"

I hesitated.

She cupped her hand over my ear. "I know you won't let me ride you. I just have to tell you something."

"OK," I said. I wiped my sweaty face on my new purple soccer shirt and, waving to both Dex and Lou, ran with her toward the bike rack. Both boys stopped walking and stood in the middle of the girls' field, looking perplexed.

She didn't tell me anything earth-shattering at the bikes, just, "Some people are so uncoordinated." She cocked her head toward the two girls who had crashed into the goalpost earlier in practice. We both covered our mouths.

I never act like that. I hate girls who act like that. It seems so stupid and insensitive and immature. The strangest part was, I liked it.

nine

"You're not getting to be friends with Morgan Miller, are you?" Dex asked me in the morning, as I was eating my Cheerios.

"Why shouldn't I?"

He shook his head. "You've been saying for two years what a lousy friend she is to CJ, what a bad influence. She's so nasty and sarcastic. I'm just repeating what you've always said."

He was telling the truth, so what could I say? "People change," I told him. "And I'm sarcastic, too, sometimes."

"Yeah." Dex laughed. "You, sarcastic."

"You ready?" Mom asked, rushing through the kitchen with her hands above her head, braiding her shiny black hair. "Let's go, let's go!"

We piled into the car. "You smell," Dex said, tugging at my soccer shirt.

"Oh, I'm so concerned," I said.

Dex turned around and stared at me. "That *was* sarcastic. Holy."

I sneaked a sniff at myself while Dex climbed into the car. I smelled OK, I thought, but now I was nervous about it. I hoped all the other girls would be wearing their soccer shirts, too. Last year we all did. It surprised me that I would care at all what anybody else wore, and resolved not to. When we pulled up in front of school, though, I was relieved to see all the other girls wearing their soccer shirts. I sat down with Morgan, our backs against the cool brick wall in the front of school.

Dex shook his head as he passed us.

Morgan watched him go by, then whispered to me, "Look at CJ."

CJ, who can't do soccer this year because she has ballet almost every afternoon, was just about the only girl in seventh grade who wasn't in a purple Boggs Bobcats soccer shirt. CJ had on a pale yellow dress, instead. It made her skin look even greener than usual — to match her eyes. I whispered to Morgan, "What about her?"

"Exactly," Morgan answered. She laughed. The bell rang. She grabbed me by the elbow and whispered as we shuffled in, "You are so funny, Olivia. I can't believe I never knew."

I placed my lunch carefully in my locker and raised an eyebrow.

"What?" Morgan asked. "I just forgot mine."

"Your permission slip?"

"No, my lunch. It must be on the counter, that's all. Jeez." She turned and sprinted toward her homeroom.

I gathered the books I'd need for the morning and headed toward Ms. Masters's room. I passed Zoe Grandon at the water fountain. She yelled for me to wait up for her, so I did. She asked me when I was getting my braces.

"Friday," I told her.

She scrunched her face sympathetically.

"The orthodontist told me my teeth aren't the worst he's ever seen."

"Oh," said Zoe. "That's a sort of horrible thing to say."

I nodded. "I asked him if the other person survived."

Zoe laughed out loud as we walked into Ms. Masters's room. Ms. Masters put her finger to her lips. Zoe covered her mouth with both hands and whispered to me, "You're funny."

"So I hear," I mumbled to myself.

All through the pledge I stole glances over at Zoe. She is very friendly, but I never know what to talk about with her. Her broad face is so open and eager, so ready to laugh along with anything you come up with, it seems almost nasty to be at a loss for topics of discussion with her. She couldn't be nicer or easier to get along with, and yet there's always something that makes me turn away from her. And it's not just that Morgan was giving Zoe the Silent Treatment. I make my own judgments.

Zoe glanced over at me right before the bell rang and caught me looking at her. She smiled. I smiled back.

Last Friday, Tommy Levit flicked Zoe's bra strap a number of times, such an immature little jerk, and when he wouldn't stop, she let him have it verbally with an expression I would never use, but which I thought was totally justified, and which I have memorized in case someday I wear a bra and somebody flicks it. But somehow Morgan and CJ twisted the whole thing all around and made Zoe apologize to Tommy, saying the incident was her own fault because she was wearing a tight shirt. It was ridiculous and insulting. Zoe looked so confused. I tried to tell her she shouldn't apologize at all, that she was absolutely not in the wrong — but she caved in to the peer pressure of the more popular girls and left me sitting alone. I'm not really friends with the boys (except now I guess Lou), so I suppose I wasn't the right one to listen to on how to deal with them, but anyway since then I've felt like, for all Zoe's big size and outgoing nature, she isn't a very strong person. I try not to be so judgmental, but sometimes I can't help myself.

Zoe headed to French and I went to Spanish. Morgan caught up with me halfway and asked if I'd done the homework. Of course I had. I didn't ask if she'd done it because I didn't want to be in the position of her asking to copy mine. We took our seats. She looked especially sad. "You OK?" I asked her.

She nodded, then rested her head in her crossed arms on her desk. I got the homework all right, but I didn't volunteer and didn't get chosen. When the bell rang, I gathered my books and stood up to walk to math/science with Morgan, but Lou gripped me by the shoulder. "Hey," he said.

Morgan continued walking with a scowl on her face. I couldn't tell if she was angry at me or what, but Lou wasn't letting go of my shoulder. I looked up into his red-cheeked face.

"Um, your shirt is nice," he said.

"My shirt?"

"The soccer ball. Is nice. And the, um, fit."

I looked down at the shirt that hung straight down from my shoulders to the middle of my thighs. It fit me about like everything else fits me. "Thanks," I said. The boys' uniforms hadn't come in yet, so Lou was wearing a blue button-down with the sleeves rolled up. I told him his shirt was nice, too. We sounded like a couple of idiots.

"Um," he said. "I was wondering."

That's all. I stood waiting to hear what he was wondering, but instead of talking he just turned redder and redder until he was almost purple. Señora Goldsmith called from behind her desk to ask if he was OK, if he wanted a pass to the nurse, because he looked like he had a fever.

"No, *gracias*," he said, his voice cracking, and pushed me out the door. We walked toward math / science. "I . . ." he started.

I switched my books to the arm between us and kept walking.

"I . . ." he said again.

We had reached the door of Ms. Cress's room. Ms. Cress was at the board, reaching up to write some equations in chalk. All the boys spend the whole double period of math and science staring at Ms. Cress's long, shapely, pale legs in their high-heeled boots. I saw Lou look.

"Lou!" Tommy Levit yelled. Lou flicked his head toward the front corner where Tommy was standing, with his hands in his pockets.

"Here," Lou said to me, and thrust a folded piece of paper at me. I took it and went to my desk, put down my books, and unfolded the note. It was a cartoon Lou had drawn in pencil, of two dogs standing in front of a toilet. The smaller one looks perplexed and disappointed as the bigger one tells him, *I know I used to like drinking out of it, too — but I've moved on.*

I smiled at it, and looked up to watch Lou walk over to Tommy. Dex has a point; Lou does sort of walk with a *de-doe, de-doe* rhythm, and his hair goes in many directions. You could see why people think he's goofy, especially compared to somebody like Tommy Levit, with his dimples and squashed-in cute face, and his solid way of moving — shoulders square, eyes straight ahead. Lou's eyes never stop darting around. I watched him arching down to listen to Tommy. I felt myself melting a little at how apologetic Lou looks. *He's a geek,* I heard inside my head. But then I congratulated myself on resisting those messages. I reread the cartoon. So cute. My palms got damp. It felt weird but good.

Behind me, I heard CJ whispering to Zoe.

"What?" Zoe gasped.

CJ whispered to her some more. I kept sitting

straight in my seat, telling myself to mind my own business. I folded the cartoon, put it in my back pocket, took out my math notebook, and rechecked my problems. They were all right, and I couldn't stand it anymore, so I turned around to see what was happening. Zoe was slumped down into her seat, looking like she'd just been given devastating news. I've never seen her look so pale and horrified.

"What happened?" I asked Zoe.

CJ answered, "Nothing."

Zoe opened her mouth, said nothing, then dropped her head down hard onto her desk. In my mind, I started reviewing what my father had taught me about CPR.

Meanwhile, Morgan had gone over to CJ's desk and was leaning toward her, whispering, "You think you're so special, don't you?"

CJ shook her head.

"What happened?" I asked again.

"Nothing!" CJ yelled. Ms. Cress looked at us over her shoulder, then went back to writing on the board.

"She's fixing up Zoe with Lou," Morgan told me.

"Lou?" I asked.

"Do you even like Lou?" she asked Zoe.

Without raising her face off the desk, Zoe shook her head. The bell rang, and Ms. Cress asked everybody to sit. Lou straggled back to his seat without looking at me. I didn't know what to do, or think. *What if he likes her, too? Everybody likes Zoe; he probably will.* I started to stand up, but since I had no plan of where to go, I sat back down. I pushed my pencil onto my notebook page and broke the tip, which spoiled the clean copied-over homework with a dark smudge. *Pull yourself together,* I told myself. My palms were drenched.

Morgan leaned close to CJ and whispered, "Not everybody needs a boyfriend. You just think you're so great to have a boyfriend, and be a little ballerina, in your ballerina dress, so much better than the rest of us."

CJ looked pleadingly at me, her oldest friend. She was starting to cry, I could tell by the way she pulled her lips inside her mouth. I decided to check my math problems again — thank goodness for math, problems with actual answers.

"You go ahead," I heard Morgan whisper to CJ. "Do everything you can to set yourself apart. I hope you're impressed with yourself, Superstar. The rest of us will be perfectly happy to stick together in the shadows."

I wished there were some shadows for me to hide in.

Ms. Cress asked Morgan to sit down, so she did.

When we split up to work on our codes, I asked for a pass to go to the bathroom. By the time I got back, we were up to going over the homework, thank goodness. I was called on to go to the board a few minutes later. I didn't even know what problem we were up to. That's never happened to me before. When I looked back at the class from up in front, Zoe's head was on her desk, CJ's face was buried in her palms, Morgan was staring lockjawed at the clock, Lou had his desk opened and was hiding inside it, and Tommy Levit was scrunched so far down in his chair he looked like he might slither out under his desk. Ms. Cress made some joke about marking us all absent for the day. Nobody laughed. I turned back to the board, tried to concentrate, forgot to carry the one, and got the problem wrong.

ten

As we set the dinner table, Dex made the mistake of asking, "How's Lou?"

I slammed the stack of plates onto the table, which startled me for a second, long enough to gasp, but when I saw nothing had chipped I returned immediately to being furious. "Not everybody needs a boyfriend."

"What?" Dex asked. "What's wrong with you?"

I took one of the plates and set it down hard in front of Mom's place. "Nothing! Why does it always have to be something wrong with me? Maybe there's something wrong with you!"

I slammed a plate down in front of my place.

"Are you crying?" Dex asked.

I wasn't, but that started me. I ran to my room and slammed the door shut. I was feeling persecuted and overwhelmed — why would CJ fix up Zoe with my — whatever — my crush? Obviously, she didn't know, but I still felt like, I wouldn't do that to her. I'm such a good friend to CJ, I defend her all the time, I am so there for her and happy for her successes — I made her a flip book for being in *The Nutcracker* last year, a ballerina doing a leap and a pirouette, and it took me a solid month, and she barely even thanked me for it. Even though she's the first to act annoyed with me when I use words she thinks are fancy, or make fun of me in a group of friends when I do or say something she thinks is less than cutting-edge cool, even with all that, I have always been totally loyal to her, my first friend. But enough is enough. She has no right to stab me in the back. I have plenty of dirt I could tell Morgan, and CJ would deserve all of it. I wouldn't, of course, but it's totally unfair that she can be mean and callous about my feelings without the slightest thought that, you know what? I could do damage to you, too.

I lay down on my bed with my feet up on the wall. I wasn't crying anymore. I forced myself to imagine Lou and Zoe walking down the hall together, holding hands. That got the tears going again, until I reminded myself, *That won't happen, because he can't go out with anybody, and Zoe doesn't even like him.* Why doesn't Zoe like him? What's so wrong with him? He's smart and kind and screw her, the Grand One — she doesn't deserve somebody so good. Was I missing some horrible fact about him? Maybe he really is a loser. Why haven't I told anybody I like him? Am I really just private? Or is it shame, because of other people's opinions? Am I turning into someone who does only what the crowd allows?

I tumbled off my bed, sat down at my desk, picked up my phone, and dialed Lou's number. I hung up before it rang. *Do I need a boyfriend?* I asked myself. *Am I such a weak girl that I need a boyfriend to feel like I have value as a person?* Yuck. I hate girls like that.

I don't need a boyfriend. I don't need anybody. I have always been really proud of my self-sufficiency. I listen to my own heart, my own mind, march to my own drummer. I'm my own person, standing alone. Anyway, can I still stick together with my best friend in the shadows if I have a boyfriend? *My best friend.* I liked the sound of that.

Mom called me to dinner.

"One minute!" I yelled back. I picked up my phone again and quickly dialed Morgan's number. When she answered, I whispered into the phone, "I can't talk, they're all at the dinner table, I just wanted to say that . . ."

"Who is this?" Morgan asked.

I rested my forehead in my palm. "Olivia. Pogostin."

She laughed. "I know."

"Oh." I closed my eyes. "I just wanted you to know I think what you said to CJ was totally justified. I think she really deserved that."

"Oh, good," Morgan said. "You didn't say anything to me the rest of the day and all through soccer, so I sort of thought . . ." She didn't finish.

"Thought what?"

"Thought . . ." she repeated. "I thought you were mad at me."

"I wasn't," I told her. "I was just in shock."

"Because of what CJ did, fixing up Zoe and Lou, you mean?"

"Yeah." *Should I tell her?* "Remember what we were saying, about Lou?"

"I know it! What is it with Lou Hochstetter this week? As if!"

I just breathed and didn't tell her. It felt dishonest but also safer.

"And the note? Could you believe that one?"

"Note?" I asked, nervously. "What note?"

"You know. CJ passed that note to Tommy saying forget about fixing up Zoe and Lou. Remember? She told us at the lockers, after seventh period?"

"Oh, yeah." I shook my head. "But . . ."

"I don't think that makes up for it."

"No," I agreed. "Completely insufficient."

"What?" Morgan asked.

"That was completely insufficient," I said louder.

"Yeah," Morgan agreed. "Well, she's been like that ever since she got friendship rings with Zoe Grandon."

"Like what?"

"What you said before."

I wasn't sure what she meant so I said, "Oh."

"Not that I care that they got friendship rings together."

"No," I agreed. "Why would you?"

"Right," said Morgan. "It's a free country, although those are the most boring ugly rings, if you ask me."

"But nobody did."

"Did what?"

"Ask you," I said.

"True," said Morgan.

"That was a joke. I was being sarcastic."

"I know." She forced out a laugh. "You really are funny. Much funnier than CJ. We'd never get friendship rings, you and me. Too, whatever. Corny. Right?"

"I don't know," I said. I honestly thought the rings CJ and Zoe had gotten together were sort of pretty, in an understated way, and had even imagined that maybe someday Morgan and I might get rings together, too. "I guess we definitely wouldn't."

"Why?" Morgan asked. "Would you want to?"

"Oh, no," I told her. "I think something like friend-ship rings just makes whoever doesn't have them feel hurt and left out."

"Mmm-hmm," Morgan answered.

"Which wouldn't be moral of us at all, right?" I lay across my bed with my feet on the wall and my head hanging backward. "Besides, we don't need . . ."

"CJ is very needy."

"Olivia!" Dad yelled. "Now!"

"I gotta go," I said. "I just wanted you to know that I agreed with you, that CJ did the wrong thing, today."

"Thanks," Morgan whispered back. "I'm glad you called."

"Hey, what are friends for?" I said.

"Beats the crap out of me," Morgan said.

"What does?"

"What friends are for."

"It was a rhetorical question," I explained.

"A what?"

"It's . . . There's not an answer."

"Welcome to my world," Morgan said.

"Olivia!"

"I gotta go," I told her.

" 'Bye." She hung up before I did.

eleven

"So? Tell me what's going on." Mom stooped to check the date on a carton of milk. "You've seemed preoccupied, the past couple of days."

I gripped the grocery cart handle and didn't answer. We do the shopping together, Thursday nights. It's our special time.

Mom placed a half gallon of milk in the cart and chewed on her thumb as she read over her list. "Do we need toilet paper?" Two cute guys, in their twenties maybe, passed us just as she asked that. The taller one smiled at me. I looked down at my Adidas. Mom tugged the cart toward the paper aisle. "We always need toilet paper."

"Mom?"

She turned around, holding an eight-pack of toilet paper. "What, sweetheart?"

"I like Lou Hochstetter."

"I had a feeling that might be it." Mom smiled at me. She tossed the toilet paper into the cart. "He sounds like a nice boy."

"He is," I whispered. I could feel my face heating up. "I'm allowed to go out with somebody, right? We're not, I'm not. He, well, I'm just wondering, for the future."

"I trust you implicitly, Olivia," Mom said as we turned the corner at the head of the aisle. "You're smart and responsible, and when you feel ready to go out with somebody, I know you'll handle it wisely and with self-respect."

"That's what I thought," I said. "I will, don't worry."

"I don't." Mom leaned against the grocery cart. "I'm happy for you. That's exciting."

I smiled.

She chose three cans of tuna, then said, "Tell me about Morgan."

"Why? What did Dex say?"

"Just that he's concerned. He says you two have become inseparable."

"Really?" I surprised myself by smiling at that. "I know what you think about her, Mom, from what you heard through CJ's mother. And me."

Mom pulled a store coupon out of the dispenser and held it without reading it. "I know what you've always thought of her."

"Morgan says I'm her best friend."

"Are you?"

"I don't know," I answered. "I don't even know what that means."

"Well?" Mom crumpled the coupon and threw it in the cart. "Do you like her? Do you have things in common? Do you . . ."

"She's the prettiest, nastiest, angriest, most powerful, and most vulnerable girl in seventh grade. I'm none of those things. Well, except girl and seventh grader."

"And pretty." Mom smiled. "She seems very different from you."

"That's true, but you don't know her, Mom. She's been having a hard time, this past week. You know how her father left and moved to California? He's not sending the family any money, again. She tries to act tough but she's really scared, I think. And . . ."

"And?"

"And she's fun." I shrugged. "When she talks to me,

it's like I'm the only person in the world. I don't know. I can't explain."

"I had a friend like that," Mom said, closing her eyes slowly.

"Really?"

Mom nodded. "Colleen Lusardi. She went to the parochial school down the road, and she looked so wholesome, the long blond hair and clear blue eyes, white socks and crisp linen uniform, I was afraid she'd be too boring for me. I was listening to jazz and writing self-indulgent poetry at the time. I thought I was a rebel. But Colleen. I was deceived by her appearance, to say the least. Colleen was wild, impulsive — she'd do anything and laugh. She was so unlike me, but at the same time, she was also like me — like the hidden, inside part of me nobody ever knew about. Nana hated her."

"I bet," I said, throwing a box of Cheerios into the cart. "Nana thinks *I'm* impulsive."

Mom laughed. "I know."

"What did she do?" I asked. "Colleen, I mean. What did you do with her?"

"Oh, I don't know." Mom placed a box of All-Bran beside the Cheerios.

"Come on," I prodded.

"Colleen. She used to, OK. She wanted to smoke

cigarettes in my car, and I wouldn't let her — I hated
cigarettes even then, and my father would've taken
that car away in a second if he ever smelled smoke in
it — so Colleen, one night she wouldn't wait till we
got to the party we were going to, maybe ten minutes
away. She stood up on my car seat and hung out the
window from the waist up. Smoking and singing. An
Allman Brothers song, I think."

"That sounds really dangerous."

"Oh, it was ridiculous." Mom picked up the box of
All-Bran and looked at it again. "I actually hate this
stuff."

I smiled. "Put it back."

She put it back on the shelf and grinned at me.

"You let her hang out the window?" I asked. "You
won't even let me sit in the front seat with a seat belt
on."

"I know. Can you believe it?"

"I would never do that," I promised. "Anything like
that. I'm careful."

"I know you are. Good."

"I can't even imagine you . . ."

"It was crazy." Mom shook her head. "She was fun.
I was fun, with her. For a little while we were best
friends."

"Where is she now?" I asked. My mother doesn't

talk about herself as a teenager much. She mostly talks about books. It felt weird and exciting, as if she were a new girl moving into town. She seemed new.

"I don't know," Mom said. "Should we get bananas? Let's get some bananas."

I followed her out to the fruit area. "You lost touch? Did you have a fight? Did Nana forbid you to see her?"

"No." Mom placed a bunch of greenish bananas carefully into the front section of our cart. "Nothing so dramatic. We were different. I went on to Yale. Colleen, I don't know. She had other interests. I didn't agree with some of her choices, so I guess I pulled away. We weren't very much alike." Mom picked up a string bean, snapped it in half, took a bite, and nodded.

I ripped a plastic bag off the roll, massaged it open, and held it up for Mom to fill. When the bag was loaded, I asked, "Do you miss her? Colleen?"

"Miss her?" Mom looked up into the ceiling light and smiled. "Sometimes, maybe. I wouldn't be friends with her now. It's not who I am, but . . ."

"What?" I asked.

"There's a part of me that she discovered, or that I discovered with her, and I guess I'm grateful for the discovery."

I nodded. "I know what you mean."

"Just be careful," Mom said. "And make sure you keep thinking for yourself, OK?"

"I will," I promised. "I always do."

"That's what I like to hear." She took the handle of the cart and pushed it to the check-out area. I followed her.

twelve

The next day, Friday, Lou told me in math that he'd had a breakthrough on our code project. He asked if I'd come up with something, and I had to admit I hadn't done any work on it at all. Usually I do most of the work in a group project, so as he began to explain his concept, I didn't pay much attention — I was too busy insulting myself over what a distracted, lazy ditz I was becoming. When he said, "It's elegant, don't you think?" I had to ask him to repeat his idea. It was to take the symbols above the numbers on the computer keyboard and use them in the numbers' place. "Easy to remember, and I don't think Ms. Cress will crack it that quick, especially if she's not at her keyboard."

I had to admit it was very clever. He had written down the numbers and their symbols. We played around with it, and it worked very well. We were both psyched, and started discussing making up a letter code, too. When the bell rang and Morgan grabbed me, I was startled.

Lou watched me go backward out of the classroom.

"We'll work on it more later," I yelled to him.

"I can't believe you got stuck with him," Morgan said as she slammed her locker shut.

"He's really smart," I said.

She made a gagging face and jiggled my lock while she waited for me to organize my books and take out my lunch. "I'm on a diet," she whispered. "I tossed mine in the garbage on the way this morning."

I asked her why. She looked very skinny to me.

She pinched skin on her waist — there was barely enough to grip. "You wouldn't understand," she told me.

"You're right, I don't," I told her, pulling my lunch down from the shelf of my locker. "You're the prettiest girl in seventh grade. I don't understand why you wouldn't eat lunch. That just seems self-destructive to me."

Morgan let out a burst of air and smiled.

"What?"

She shook her head. "Sometimes I don't know whether to say *thank you* or *screw you* to you."

I closed my locker and locked it. She'd have to figure out what she wants to say to me, herself.

She grumbled, "Come on. Hurry."

"What's the rush?"

She grabbed me by the elbow and pulled me toward the cafeteria. "Don't you hate walking in there late, feeling like everybody is watching you?"

"I never thought about it," I admitted. "Why would they watch us?"

"Judging," she answered.

As we crossed the cafeteria, I peeked around to see who might be judging us. Lou smiled at me from his table near the front and started to stand up. "I thought of another thing we could add to the code!"

I looked away. Out of my peripheral vision I saw him sink back down in his seat.

Everybody else seemed too engrossed in their own lunches and conversations to take any notice of us. I looked for Dex. There were a few eighth-grade girls leaning on a table with their backs to me and their hips shifted sideways. Dex was probably sitting opposite them.

Zoe Grandon smiled at us and waved, then pointed

at a space next to her that was vacant. CJ wasn't with her. I looked around quickly for CJ, surprised to see her unattached from Zoe. She'd been Zoe's shadow all week. It occurred to me that maybe Zoe was angry at CJ over the Lou incident. It was sort of hard to picture Zoe angry. She waved again, a little more frantically.

Morgan smiled at her, let go of my elbow, and walked quickly over to the spot Zoe had been pointing to. "Where's CJ?" Morgan asked Zoe.

"I don't know," Zoe said, tucking her long blond hair behind her ears.

Morgan smiled her electric white smile at Zoe and rested her chin in her palms. I sat down opposite them and took my sandwich and pretzels and soda out of my bag. I tried to think of something to say about our homework or current events, anything but what I was thinking, which was, *Morgan is MY best friend, so quit smiling at each other like that!*

I told myself to quit focusing on insipid social issues and think of a world event or political conflict to bring up as a topic instead, but I couldn't think of any. I started insulting myself about that and then remembered how much Morgan and Zoe seem to like it when somebody insults herself so I said, "I just realized, I'm so stupid I haven't read the paper all week!"

They looked at me blankly for a minute and then they both got hysterical, thumping the table, laughing. I smiled, unsure if they were laughing at me or with me.

They kept laughing, and I was feeling increasingly uncomfortable, so I glanced around and was startled to see CJ was standing beside me, pulling a soccer shirt out of her bag. She held it up against her body as if it belonged to her. It was number five, the number she wore last year when she only had two ballet classes a week, instead of five. This year she can't play. She had made it up to performance level, a very exciting achievement for which she'd been working incredibly hard; our two families had gone out to dinner at the swim club the night she found out, to celebrate. CJ's mother, whom I call Aunt Corey even though she's not my blood aunt, was so proud of CJ that she kept squeezing CJ's arm until CJ had to excuse herself from the table and go to the ladies' room. CJ was proud, too, and so excited her cheeks were a little rosy. When I found her in the ladies' room that night, she was staring at herself in the mirror, and she told me it was the first day she'd ever allowed herself to think all her mother's dreams for her had a chance of coming true. I hugged her and told her how happy I was for her, and how confident I was about her future. She really is gifted and dedicated. She deserves her success.

So I wasn't sure what to make of the fact that she was holding a soccer jersey. She smiled nervously, and nodded slightly.

"But . . ." I said.

"You . . ." said Morgan.

She climbed onto the bench and sat down next to me. I moved my lunch over a little to make room for hers. My tuna fish was sticking to the roof of my mouth. I put it down on top of the lunch bag, and when I saw Morgan staring at it, I happily pushed it toward her. She took a bite and put it back down. I hoped she'd finish it. I get angry when I see girls trying to be so skinny they're barely there. What kind of culture do we live in?

CJ opened her lunch bag, looked in, and said casually, "I just decided I'd rather be on the soccer team."

"Rather than what?" I asked her.

"Rather than dance."

"You're quitting dance?"

"No need to alert the media," she said in the snottiest voice she'd ever used. I turned to her, surprised. "Or your mother," she added.

I felt myself getting angry, as I always do when she tries to humiliate me publicly. I took a deep breath and asked, "Well, what did *your* mother say? She must be devastated."

OK, that was mean, a low blow, since I knew that of course her mother would be devastated. CJ's ballet career is her mother's dream come true, and I knew that better than any of the other girls at the table. But I couldn't help myself from giving CJ that dig, after she was so snide to me.

CJ shrugged. "It's my decision."

Of course she was right. I took a sip of my soda to avoid having to acknowledge her point.

"When did you realize that?" Morgan asked her.

"Yesterday," CJ said.

Morgan smiled at CJ. I gulped more soda. I felt totally miserable, with no idea why; like I might start punching somebody if they all weren't careful.

"She's disappointed, of course," CJ said, opening her yogurt. "She said she wished I felt differently, but that I have to do what's right for me."

CJ turned to me. I had to look her in the eyes, her wide, vulnerable green eyes, which were flicking around my face, begging for approval. "Well," I said. What could I say? As talented as she is, she was also right — it was her decision. It might not be the choice I'd have made in her position, but I had to respect her for following her own conscience. Sometimes she seems so eager to please her mother she forgets to be a person, herself. "Congratulations," I told her.

"Thanks," CJ said gratefully. "And I'm coming apple picking, too."

Morgan's head snapped up to look at CJ. "You are?" she asked.

I unwrapped my box of pretzel sticks to keep from reminding Morgan she had already asked me to sit with her. Last year when we went to the waste disposal plant, I didn't care one single bit who I sat with. I think I ended up with Gabriela Shaw one way and Roxanne Luse the other, and I read a book the whole time. It was strange to me that I cared, this year — cared a lot, honestly.

I shoved the box of pretzels at Morgan, who took some and smiled gently at me. I looked away and offered some pretzels to Zoe, who usually grabs a handful but this time she shook her head. I held the box in front of CJ, who never accepts. This time she did.

"I handed in my permission slip today," she told us proudly, and took a loud bite of the three pretzel sticks.

I felt like I should say something to her. "I was wondering why your name was finally erased from Ms. Cress's board," I managed.

"That's why," she answered.

Morgan blew the bangs away from her eyes. "I guess we won't be having a class trip to see you in *The Nutcracker* this year, then," she said to CJ.

CJ's smile sunk a little.

Morgan crumpled my lunch bag and tossed it over me and CJ into the garbage can. We all watched it arc in perfectly. Then she leaned toward me and whispered, "You ready to go outside?"

I shoved the last bunch of pretzels into my mouth and nodded as I chewed them and stood up, all at the same time. I tried to think of something else to say to CJ, but nothing came to mind.

"As if you'd tell your mother," Morgan muttered to me as I hurried after her, down the hall.

"My mother probably knows already," I said. "They talk every day."

"Some people," Morgan started, but then said, "Forget it," and pushed out the door. She paced around the perimeter of the playground, dragging her fingers along the metal fence. She hung her head, hiding her eyes behind her bangs, and pushed her lower jaw forward, not saying a word. I started chattering like a bimbo, but I couldn't help myself. I knew I was acting foolish, the way CJ used to — hustling to keep up the pace with Morgan, complimenting her, asking her if she was OK. She ignored me and when the bell rang, sprinted in alone.

In English/social studies, I passed her a second note when she didn't answer my first, assuring her I wasn't planning on saying anything to my mother in case that's what she was mad about. I was annoying myself, not to mention Morgan.

We were in different groups for gym, which gave me a rest from pursuing her, and I spent the time berating myself — *Have a little self-respect, would you, please?* — but after, when we were changing in the locker room, unable to stop myself, I slid over next to her. "If you want to talk . . ." I said.

Obviously she didn't want to talk because if she wanted to talk she would talk.

"I'm here," I added, in case somehow she'd managed not to notice.

She turned her back to me and took off her white gym top and in the same motion, pulled on her blue shirt. I considered telling her it was a nice shirt, but miraculously exercised my first moment of self-restraint in over two hours and stood up instead, and went back to my own locker. She slammed her locker shut and said, "Don't."

I turned back around. Morgan was walking toward me. Poor Gabriela Shaw, who was putting on her pants sitting on the bench between Morgan and me, pulled her long legs in and scrunched up as small as she could to get out of Morgan's way. I shrunk down into my shoulders, wondering if Morgan was about to punch me.

Morgan stood in front of me, too close, and whispered, "I'm not bringing any junk food for the trip, Monday."

I swallowed. "OK," I said.

She didn't move away, and I started wondering if I had misinterpreted what she said. She'd said it as if it would insult me, or as if it were of terrible consequence. I couldn't, as hard as I tried, think of a deep and consequential meaning of her not bringing junk food for the trip.

"It doesn't matter to me," I whispered, and then since she didn't seem to have any reaction to that, I added, "I'm getting braces this afternoon anyway so I couldn't eat junk food anyway, so I'm not bringing any either, so it really doesn't matter to me at all. Anyway."

She stood there for another few seconds, and just when I was starting to feel another big babble about to vomit itself out of my mouth, she turned away. Thank goodness. She almost knocked Gabriela off the bench again. Gabriela and I shrugged at each other. Morgan grabbed her backpack and stormed out of the locker room.

thirteen

Morgan was waiting for me outside the locker room door. "Sorry," she whispered. "I'm not great at dealing with somebody being nice to me."

I shrugged.

We walked together out to the bike rack.

"There's just," Morgan whispered to me. "There's a lot going on at my house right now. I need to talk to somebody. Not *need*, but . . ."

"You could try me," I suggested.

Morgan bent over her bike. "My mom was laid off."

"Oh," I said.

"Yeah. No big deal, you know, it's just, I can't exactly ask her for junk food money when she can't even manage lunches, if you know what I mean."

"Sure," I said. I didn't know what to do and wished I had something to give her. My own lunch gurgled around in my belly. "Oh, no. I'm really sorry I said that thing about dieting. Before. I didn't realize."

"That's OK." Morgan snapped open her bike lock. "Anyway, I don't know why I told you. It's not like I need sympathy, or anything." She blinked a few times.

I thought of touching her shoulder, but then I thought that might make her cry even more. I felt honored she was trusting me with her secret, and I didn't want to mess it up. I wasn't sure what to do.

"You won't tell anybody, right?" she asked, flicking her long hair back from her face. "Not even your mother."

I shook my head.

"Not that it matters, it's just, I'm not supposed to tell anybody."

"I won't say anything." I crossed my heart. "I swear."

"Thanks." Morgan blinked a few times and looked up at the sky.

I put my arm around her, and she leaned slightly down toward me, until her head rested on my shoulder. We stood there like that for a while.

"You're gonna be late," she said.

I gasped, yanked my arm off her, and looked at my watch. It was already three-fifteen; I was supposed to be in the orthodontist's chair already.

"You want me to ride you?"

"No," I said. "That's OK, I don't need . . ."

"You'll be really late."

"I can walk fast."

"Fine, 'bye." She yanked her bike out of the rack.

"Hey!"

"Hey yourself," she said. "You could need me sometime, too, you know." A tear rolled down her cheek. She wiped it away with the back of her hand.

"OK," I said.

"Forget it."

"No," I said, touching the seat of her bike. "Please? I'm so late."

She wiped her nose. "Hold onto me," she said. "I won't let you fall. Don't worry."

I climbed onto her bike as she held it steady. I glanced around, hoping my brother was long gone. My toes just reached the pavement. I leaned forward to hold the handlebars while Morgan unhooked the helmet and held it out to me.

"No," I protested. "It's yours. You should wear it."

She placed the helmet on my head. "I never do."

"You should. It's really unsafe . . ."

"Don't tell me what to do." She tightened the strap under my chin. "I have a hard head, really." She turned away and hiked her right leg over the crossbar. "A thick skull and small brain."

I wiggled the helmet to fit better over my pigtails. "I don't feel great about this," I told her. "What would my mom say?"

"Not that she'll ever know," Morgan said. "CJ tells her mother everything."

I buckled my helmet under my chin and fiddled with the strap.

"Her mother is one of the things that came between me and her. Mothers don't like me."

I swallowed. "Mine does."

"I wasn't fishing for compliments. Even my own mother doesn't like me much. Hold my waist," she said. "And just lean with me."

"OK." I didn't know where to put my feet so I held them straight out.

"Just relax," she yelled as she started pedaling. "You have to trust me."

"I do," I insisted. We were coming up to the curb so I yelled, "Careful!"

She jerked her head toward me. We toppled off the bike onto the road. No cars were coming, luckily. Her knee was skinned, but otherwise we were both fine.

"Sorry," I said, disentangling myself from her bike.

"Don't do that," she scolded, lifting it off the ground.

"Maybe this is too dangerous."

"You have to just go with me, let me watch out. Can you do that?"

"I'll try." We got on again. I gripped her waist with my hands — she felt very solid. I, on the other hand, was shaking. As we rounded the corner at the end of the circle, she leaned into the turn, but I felt like we were about to capsize again so I leaned the other way and over we went.

"You have to lean *with* me," she repeated. "Stop trying to steer!"

"I can't help it."

"Then we're just going to keep landing on the pavement!"

"Maybe I should ride you," I suggested. "It might be easier for me, that way."

"My bike's too big for you," she pointed out.

"I could just walk. It's OK if I'm a few minutes late."

"Fine."

"Want to walk with me?"

She shrugged.

"That would be great," I said pleadingly. "Please?"

I walked along the curb, and she walked on the sidewalk, with the bike between us.

fourteen

The next morning, I found her barefoot on my front porch.

Her knees were propped under her chin and her tan arms were wrapped tight around her muscular legs. Her long, shiny hair fell over her eyes. She was rocking slightly while she waited. Anybody else would've rung the doorbell.

I had wandered into the kitchen and found Dex, standing in his boxer shorts and staring out the window as the water overflowed the glass he was holding under the tap. He's an environmentalist, so it was unlike him to be wasting water. "What are you doing?" I asked him, and looked out to the front porch, where he was focused.

"How long has she been there?" I asked Dex.

He turned off the water and took a sip from his glass, still staring out the window at her. "Don't know," he answered.

We stood beside each other staring out at her for another minute. Dex finished his water and placed the glass in the sink. Water is the only beverage he'll drink. People think he's so easygoing, but actually he's just charming. He has a great smile, slow and knowing, which makes people think he's carefree. He flashed it at me. "Should we rescue her?" he asked, drying his hand on his hair.

"She's not a kitten," I answered, and padded over to the front door, my tube socks muffling my footsteps on the white tiles of the entrance hall. Dex's bare feet slapped along behind me. We use the back door, usually, so it took me a minute to fumble with the front door lock.

She didn't jump or gasp when I sat down next to her on the top step. "How long have you been here?" I asked.

"Are you busy?" she asked.

"No." I pulled my knees up into the big gray sweatshirt I'd slept in.

"If you're busy, I could go," she said.

I looked back at Dex, who was leaning against the

open front door, standing there in just his boxer shorts. "Yes?" I asked him.

"Aren't you gonna invite her in?"

Morgan turned to look at him. Her sandals, neatly aligned, sat between us. I touched the black strap on the one closer to me and asked her, "You want to come in?"

She shrugged, slowly looking away from Dex. "Nah."

"Why did you come over?" I asked her.

"How are the braces?" she whispered.

"They kill," I admitted. "It took all afternoon, yesterday, getting them on, and I haven't been able to eat since."

"They don't look too bad." She glanced back at Dex. He smiled his slow smile, then stepped inside and closed the door softly.

I drew my breath in hard, to gather my spit, which was a major new challenge with the braces.

Mom pushed the door open and peeked out. "Oh, hi, Morgan," she said. "I didn't know you were here. What a day, huh? Can you believe I have to spend it at the museum?" She stepped out onto the porch with her shoes dangling from one hand and her yellow pocketbook looped over her shoulder. She sighed, looking up at the sky through her wire-rimmed glasses, then sat down on the porch swing. As she leaned back, she lifted her shiny black braid out of the way and draped it over her shoulder. "Ugh," she grunted, settling in. "So? What's new?"

Morgan looked at me.

"Nothing," I answered.

"How are you, Morgan?" Mom asked her. "How's your mother doing?"

I shrugged at Morgan and shook my head. I hadn't said anything to Mom about Morgan's mother. Mom was just being polite.

"Fine, thank you, Dr. Pogostin," Morgan mumbled. My mom has a Ph.D., but most people just call her Betsy.

"Send her my regards," Mom told Morgan. "Oh, what a day. You girls don't want to come to the museum, do you?" She wiggled her shoes onto her feet.

"No, thanks," I said. "We were, um, thinking maybe we'd go to, um, Sundries."

"Oh, right," Mom said. "I forgot, you said something about wanting to get some junk food for the bus ride. Here." She reached into her pocketbook and pulled out a twenty. "Bring me change, please, miss," she told me.

I was so embarrassed. I took the money and folded it quickly. "I will," I told her. "I probably can't eat any, anyway."

"Maybe some sucking candy. Right, Morgan?"

"Right," Morgan mumbled.

Mom stood up, came over, and kissed me. "'Bye, sweetheart. Have fun. 'Bye, Morgan. Make sure Olivia doesn't just get healthy food, huh? So responsible." She smiled and went back inside.

"I didn't say anything," I swore to Morgan.

She held her feet in her hands.

"I didn't!" I shook her by the knee. "Trust me."

"I believe you," she said.

"Good," I said. "Did you eat breakfast?"

She glared at me.

"Because I didn't," I explained. "Want some oatmeal? I'm starving."

"Me, too," she said.

She followed me into the kitchen. I heated some water in the kettle, emptied two envelopes of instant oatmeal into bowls, and placed them on the table. She nibbled at the dried apples in her bowl while she waited. After I poured the water in, she said, "Your hair looks good like that."

I touched my hair. "It doesn't know what ethnicity to be."

"It must be so . . . cool," Morgan said, swallowing a big mouthful of oatmeal.

"What?"

"Being, you know — having . . . ethnicities. What you said. I'm boring, just Irish and English. Nothing."

I sat down next to her. She watched me. I knew it was my turn to insult myself, to make it an even exchange. "My nose is so wide," I said tentatively. "And I hate my lips."

"You have nice lips!" Morgan pulled a napkin from the holder on the table and wiped her own mouth. "What's wrong with your lips?"

I took a napkin, too. "They're almost the same color as my skin, and thin."

"You're lucky," she said. "My mouth is too big for my face." She opened her mouth wide to demonstrate.

"At least you have straight teeth." I opened my mouth and showed my new hardware.

"You'll get used to them soon," Morgan assured me. "It's amazing what a person can get used to."

I smiled at her, and we finished our breakfast. She washed the dishes while I got dressed and tugged my hair into pigtail braids. Then we walked slowly to Sundries. It was the first time, really, that I felt totally relaxed with Morgan. It really felt like we were best friends. I kicked her a rock and she kicked it back. I decided that someday when I look back, this was a moment I should remember in my life. We walked along in rhythm with each other, our legs stepping in unison, like soldiers' legs.

As we got to the strip, Morgan asked, "Can you believe CJ?"

"That she quit dance?" I asked, slurping again.

"Unbelievable," Morgan said. "Not you. Don't worry about it. I mean, CJ. I can't believe she really quit ballet."

"What a waste," I agreed. "She was born to be a ballerina."

I pulled open the door of Sundries and held it for her. She walked past me, her sandals thwacking against the tile floor. I followed her up the toy aisle, straight to the back where the cards are.

"It's the Grand One," Morgan whispered. "I think she's a bad influence on CJ." Her lower jaw slipped a little forward, and she narrowed her eyes. "Her and Tommy, both."

Morgan was looking through the birthday and anniversary cards, lifting one after another out of the rack, opening each partway, reading it, then carefully replacing it in the rack. She didn't look amused by any of them. In fact, from the look of grim determination on her face, they might as well have been division flash cards. I read a few myself. Out of the corner of my eye, I thought I saw Morgan wiping her eyes.

"You OK?" I asked. I slurped the spit back into my mouth and thought about the two Tylenols in my pocket. I wasn't supposed to take them for another hour. My mouth ached so terribly I didn't know how I was going to make it.

She said, "Fine," but then sniffed.

"You like Tommy Levit, don't you?" I whispered. "You can tell me. Is that why you're mad at CJ? For going out with him?"

"No," she grunted. "Tommy is a jerk. And so is CJ. They deserve each other. They don't want to be with me? I don't want to be with them. Who needs 'em, right?"

"Right."

"I'm looking for a card for you. For getting your braces."

"Really?"

"How about 'Good luck in your new home'?" She held out a card with some mice carrying suitcases from one hole in the wall to another.

I smiled. She put it back and pulled out another.

"How about 'I'll miss you'? I could address it to your teeth."

I laughed. "My teeth might appreciate that," I said, which made her laugh, too. She bent her head so that her silky hair fell over my face, as we laughed together. She and CJ used to laugh like that, all last year, both of them tangled up in Morgan's shiny hair. I'd watched them over the tops of my books, sometimes.

"'Sorry for your loss,'" Morgan read from a soft-focus sympathy card, and we cracked up again. "'Please know I'm here for you at this most difficult time,'" she read.

I pushed my lower lip away from the bottom braces with my tongue, and covered my mouth with my hand. I looked up, searching for a thank you card to read Morgan in response, but instead I saw CJ and Zoe, standing near the checkout counter, staring back at us.

fifteen

They both waved. Morgan and I waved back. After a few seconds, CJ and Zoe started walking toward us.

"Don't say anything," Morgan whispered to me.

"At all?" I whispered back.

Morgan laughed silently and shoved me lightly. "You're so funny," she whispered, her hand cupped around my ear.

CJ asked me how my braces were. I wasn't sure if I was supposed to be literally silent, so I just opened my lips to display the glinting evidence.

"Wow," Zoe said. "Does it hurt?"

"It killed, getting them on," I answered. "And I can't eat anything. I'm starving." I slapped my hand over my mouth. Morgan bumped me with her shoulder. When I glanced at her, she was smirking and not looking back at me.

"Did your mother drive you guys here?" CJ asked.

I didn't say anything for a few seconds, but then I started feeling just plain rude so, with my hand still covering my mouth, I told CJ, "We walked."

"Because your mother is at the museum until three, right?"

I nodded.

"Getting psyched for apple picking?" CJ asked us, a big, fake-looking smile stretching out her pale face.

I wasn't about to answer. I just stood there with my hand over the bottom half of my face.

"We're buying some candy and stuff," Morgan said gruffly.

OK, so we weren't giving them the Silent Treatment. "Not that I can eat it," I mumbled.

"We'll buy some, too," CJ offered.

Zoe shrugged. "I'm always up for candy."

"You don't still like Tommy, do you?" Morgan asked CJ. We all looked at her for a few seconds. Morgan carefully replaced the sympathy card she'd been holding in the rack. "After yesterday?"

"What?" Zoe asked.

Morgan looked at Zoe like she was shocked. "You don't know?"

We all shook our heads.

"Even though CJ told Tommy not to fix up Zoe and Lou, he was going around the upper playground after school like, Zoe and Lou, Zoe and Lou — he was telling everybody you're after him." She shook her head at Zoe. "I thought you knew."

I stared at Morgan. I couldn't speak.

Zoe swallowed hard. I had to look away. What Morgan said was, of course, a total lie. I left school with her yesterday. She had tried riding me to the orthodontist yesterday on her bike. We didn't even see Tommy, at all.

"I-I-I . . ." CJ stuttered.

I looked up at Morgan again and waited for her to correct herself.

"It's not your fault," Morgan said to CJ. "I mean, you shouldn't have said anything to him in the first place, but once you told him to forget it, he didn't have to be such a jerk." She looked at me pleadingly.

I nodded and said, slowly, "That's just cruel."

Morgan tilted her head a little, still looking me in the eyes. I opened mine wide, trying to ESP her, *What the hell are you doing?*

Then, to my horror, I drooled. I sucked in quickly and said, "Sorry. It's really hard to control your spit when you first get braces."

"Don't worry about it," Morgan said. "We understand."

Zoe and CJ nodded.

"Thanks," I said to Morgan. "See? That's what I mean. Girls are so much nicer than boys." *Hint, hint*.

"He really did that?" Zoe asked Morgan. She looked up, her big blue eyes frightened and sad.

I turned back to Morgan, who said, "I thought you knew."

CJ and Zoe shook their heads. I shook mine, too. A week ago, I just would've said, *That's a lie!* But this week, I don't know. Morgan's my best friend, and it's complicated, but I felt like I had to wait and confront her later, privately. *Maybe I'm developing tact*, I told myself. It felt like an excuse.

"That's why I thought," Morgan said, looking down at her feet. She stopped, and I thought she might be about to tell the truth after all, and I congratulated myself on having given her the chance to do it herself. "Well," she said.

I smiled to myself.

"I figured CJ probably broke up with him," Morgan said. "I would. But, whatever."

"I'm going to," CJ said.

"Really?" Zoe asked.

I shook my head at Morgan, who sucked her lips into her mouth and looked away.

CJ stammered, "That's just, I mean, that's so cruel.

And you're my, you're more important to me, than, so . . ."

"We have to stick together," I said. *Hello!*

Morgan looked up from the ground into my eyes.

"Let's find some sucking candy," Morgan whispered.

Morgan found an eight-pack of Life Savers and asked if I liked them. I nodded. She handed them to me gently.

Zoe picked up a bag of miniature Snickers with a big sticker that said SNICKERS FUN SIZE and said, "Boy, this sure is a fun size!"

"I never had such fun," Morgan said. "Not with any other size!"

"I'm having fun already," CJ added.

"What?" I asked.

"Hey," CJ said. "I was just thinking, when you said we have to stick together or whatever?"

"What about it?" Morgan asked.

"Well," CJ said. "Zoe and I got these rings here last week, and I was thinking, wouldn't it be great if you guys got them, too?"

"I don't know," Morgan said. She put the bag of SweetTarts she'd been considering back on the shelf, and dug her fists into her hips.

"It could be like a th-th-thing," CJ said. "Like a, you know, like a bond. Between us."

"Among us," I told her. "Between is if there are only two."

"Whatever," CJ said, in an annoyed voice.

"I don't know if Zoe wants us to," Morgan said.

"Me?" Zoe asked.

How about me? I didn't ask. *Don't forget to ask me!*

Zoe smiled, but didn't look directly at anybody. "They have plenty. In a bag. Under the thing. Counter. These aren't the only two."

Morgan looked at me, her eyes scanning my face. I knew she thought the rings were boring and ugly. I knew she didn't think much of Zoe and that she and CJ weren't getting along too well anymore. Her eyebrows were raised. I couldn't tell what she wanted. I didn't know if I wanted a friendship ring at all. I was confused and angry and my mouth hurt.

Morgan shrugged.

I whispered, "Do you want to?"

"I don't have much money with me," Morgan answered.

"I have, don't worry," CJ said, quickly and happily. "You only have to put down five dollars, then it's two dollars a week, after."

"Installment," Zoe said. She picked up a bag of Hershey's Bars and put it back without really looking at it.

CJ and Morgan were grinning at each other. Zoe and I followed them up to the counter. As we tried on rings, Morgan said, "Olivia's fingers are so long and skinny, aren't they?"

Zoe and CJ both agreed. I knew I was supposed to say, *No, no, they're short and fat,* but I didn't feel like it. "This one fits," I said without smiling.

Morgan asked, "What's wrong?"

I made some excuse about my braces hurting.

"Right, sorry. Let's hurry," Morgan said.

"You have beautiful hands," Zoe told me. I looked at my hand as I waited for my mother's change, less than I'd planned to be able to give back to her, but she wouldn't mind. She'd be happy I was in a group, if that's what makes me happy. She'd be surprised, though. I never wanted to be in a group before. I wasn't even a Brownie.

The most popular group, that's what we'd be, it was obvious.

Olivia Pogostin, popular girl.

It felt peculiar even to think those words. It's not a way I've ever thought of myself. I have many goals, but *popular* has never been among them, and yet there I stood, wearing a friendship ring identical to the one being worn by the three most popular girls in seventh grade — rings that would declare our bonds of friendship, and shove our popularity in the faces of all the poor unchosens. Zoe Grandon, CJ Hurley, Morgan Miller, and, of all people, me.

sixteen

"The ring really does look good on you," Morgan told me, putting her arm around my shoulder as we walked down the sidewalk, away from Sundries.

I didn't answer.

"What's wrong?" Morgan asked.

I shrugged her arm off my shoulder. "You didn't even see Tommy after school yesterday."

"I saw him. Before you came out."

"I walked out right behind you. You were never near the upper playground."

"I meant . . ." She kicked a rock. "It was after . . . Oh, I get it." She bumped me with her shoulder. "You like Tommy."

"Tommy?" I asked. "Levit?"

"You can trust me. I won't tell anybody, if you don't want me to. CJ is breaking up with him, so he's free. Go for it. You want me to talk to him for you?"

I stopped walking. "I don't like him."

"Who *do* you like?" She looked me in the eyes.

"Nobody." I looked away, up at the stop sign at the corner. "I don't like anybody."

"Including me, obviously," Morgan said.

"You know what I mean." I couldn't face her, with my lie hanging between us. But it's not anybody's business who I like, and anyway, that wasn't the point. She was just distracting me.

She pulled the eight-pack of Life Savers out of the paper bag and offered it to me.

"No," I said. "I don't want candy. What you said made CJ feel terrible."

"You should hear some of the things CJ says about you, and you would quit being so protective of her all the time."

I shook my head and resisted my impulse to ask for details on that. "It's not just about CJ's feelings, anyway."

Morgan was unwrapping the eight-pack. "Do you like butterscotch?"

"Morgan!"

She popped a butterscotch Life Saver into her mouth. "If you don't like him, what do you care if Tommy was or wasn't saying anything about Zoe and Lou, anyway?"

"Did you see Zoe's face?"

"You have a friendship ring for half an hour and you think you're Zoe's big protector all of a sudden now, too?"

"No," I said. "That is *so* not the point," I told her.

"Oh, and what would the point be, professor?"

"Truth!"

"Oh, truth. Yes. We're all pretty lucky to have you around to keep us honest, aren't we?" She dropped to her knees and bowed down to me. "Blessed be holy Olivia, forgive us our trespasses."

"You lied," I said.

Morgan put up her hands in surrender. "Call the cops." She stood up, turned away and walked two steps, then spun back and marched toward me. "You think you're so mature. You think you're always right. Let me tell you something, Olivia. You have no clue. You think you're so much better than everybody? You're not better. You're just different. That's what everybody thinks."

I swallowed but didn't look away, and asked her as calmly as I could, "Are you talking about the color of my skin?"

"No," she said.

Neither of us moved. I didn't know whether to believe her or not.

"That's not what I meant at all," Morgan said, pushing her face forward toward mine. "I can't believe you would think that of me."

I shrugged.

"You just called me a racist, basically."

"I thought you were calling me . . . something." I blinked a few times and looked down at my sneakers. *I hope I'm the one in the wrong on this,* I thought.

Morgan jammed her fists into her hips. "Your skin is practically the same color as mine, anyway."

"So that's why I'm OK? What if I were as dark as my dad?"

She shook her head. "Do you really think I care what color your skin is?"

"If you do," I mumbled, "you're wrong to."

"I don't. I can't believe you! I can't believe you would ever think that of me. Would I have a crush on your brother if I cared about skin color?"

"You have a crush on my brother?"

"Oh, grow up," she said, stalking away from me toward the street. "Everybody has a crush on your brother."

She started crossing Oakbrook Boulevard, without looking. A car sped toward her, horn blaring. I ran after her, grabbed her and yanked her back, just before the car would've slammed into her. We fell onto the grass together. I was on top of her. I rolled off and lay on my back, catching my breath.

"You don't have to rescue me," she growled, sitting up.

I slapped the ground. "I can't do anything right!"

"No," Morgan said, standing up and dusting herself off. "You can't do anything *wrong*. That's your problem." She walked back toward the curb.

I grabbed her by the arm before she could step off and demanded, "What is that supposed to mean?"

She shook her arm out of my grasp. "Did you ever get less than an A, Olivia? Did you ever blow off preparing for a test, or take a risk, or do a stupid, reckless thing?"

"Stupid, reckless things don't seem fun to me!" I yelled. "They seem stupid. And reckless."

"Good," she said coldly. "Then you'll never get hurt. Stay safe, and alone."

I took off my new friendship ring and threw it at her feet. "I like to be alone. I don't need you. I don't need anybody."

"Obviously," she said, kicking my ring lightly. "You're right, you don't need me. You're right. Hooray for you, Olivia, you're always right."

"Here's something I got wrong," I told her with my hands on my hips. "I thought we were friends."

"Come on," Morgan said. She knelt down, picked up my ring, and placed it in the brown paper bag with the Life Savers. "Did you really think we were friends?"

I swallowed, barely trusting myself to answer without crying. "We've always been friends," I managed.

She stood up. "Now who's lying?"

I pictured being grabbed by Morgan, Monday morning, and dragged into school. I remembered how surprised I felt, all the beginning of this week. *Has it only been a week?*

"OK," I said. "Since Monday."

"Monday? Monday morning I just didn't want to walk into school alone, and you happened to be there. You didn't choose me. I barely chose you."

"You're the one who said, you wrote, you signed your note *Your best friend*. I have the note."

"Congratulations. I'll send the FBI over to get it."

"Fine," I said, clearing my throat. "So we're not friends."

She held the paper bag out to me. "You wanted the truth? There it is."

I didn't take the bag. Instead I turned my back to her and crossed the street without looking. I just had to get away from her.

A car's brakes squealed, and I saw a bright red car hurtling toward me. I stopped, squeezed my eyes closed, and waited for the impact. All my muscles cramped. But I wasn't hit. I wasn't hurt. The driver of the car driver pounded on his horn. I took a deep breath, opened my eyes, and continued across the street. I didn't look back at Morgan. I wanted to be the one walking away from her, this time.

seventeen

I walked over to Oakbrook Playground, where I used to play.

I like being alone, I reminded myself. *I walk home alone most days; it's my time for myself, when I can imagine things like what if I could fly.* I walked across the grassy area toward the swings. *Sometimes I sing show tunes in my head or even out loud, if I want. I love show tunes.* I couldn't think of a single lyric.

"I like being alone!" I said out loud. Then I cried.

I sat on the swing and wrapped my arms around the chains with my head hanging far forward, and cried, watching the tears plunk down, ineffectual little dots on the vast dry sand. "Alone," I repeated, and cried some more.

I wasn't just crying out of loneliness. That was part of it, definitely, but not all. I was mourning the loss of the girl who liked to sit here alone. I was crying about the fact that I was turning into somebody who valued having a friendship ring with the most popular clique of girls in seventh grade, turning into somebody who cares what other people think and who wants to please them, someone who wants to be liked. How weak!

I looked at my naked ring finger. For the first time in my life being alone felt lonely. I don't think I ever understood the word before.

I tried swinging a little but my heart really wasn't in it. *Holy Olivia, never wrong.* Maybe, but better that than a sheep following the crowd, bleating "I'm so stupid" all over the place. I'm not stupid and I'm proud of who I am. Mostly.

"I need a friend," I whispered. I leaned back and looked up at the sky. "I need her."

No. I don't need Morgan. I don't need anybody who lies, and walks away from me, and gets so angry, and is so fragile. Trust her? What a crazy, reckless thing to do — she was right, I don't do reckless things. It is safer to be alone.

But maybe safer shouldn't be the only consideration?

As I stood up, I covered the teardrops with sand.

eighteen

Instead of turning right, toward my house, I turned left and walked to Morgan's. I thought maybe I'd sit on her porch and wait to be discovered, like she'd done in the morning.

She was already on her deck. She was playing with a Barbie, a really tacky-looking one, which she put down behind her when she noticed me coming up her walk.

I sat down next to her and tried to think how to start. I didn't want to apologize. I just sat there for a long, long minute. *I should've thought of something on the way,* I chided myself.

She didn't say anything either. I was afraid to look at her.

I reached behind her and picked up her Barbie. I smoothed the hair down and adjusted the Velcro closure in the back of the nylon dress, then handed her to Morgan, who held her gently.

"I don't play with her anymore," Morgan mumbled.

"OK," I said. I leaned back onto my elbows and rested my hands on top of my shorts. I felt the Tylenols in their plastic bag in my pocket. My mouth was killing me, I remembered. I checked my watch. Time. "Morgan? Could I have a glass of water?"

"You? Need something from me?"

"Yeah," I said. "I do."

"Come on." She opened the screen door and held it for me. It banged shut behind us. "Shh. My mom's in bed. Depressed. Don't ask."

"OK." I followed Morgan into her kitchen, which was small and sort of triangular, with a tiny, round metal table in the corner. The cabinets were dark wood with metal handles, and reached all the way up to the ceiling. The stove had black paint peeling off it, showing silver underneath. In the sink was a pile of dirty dishes and a pot full of greasy water. A cabinet was open, and inside were two open boxes of pasta, a jar of artichoke hearts, and a can of olives. That's all. I looked at my sneakers, my shiny, white, new Adidas.

Morgan slammed that cabinet shut, climbed up on the counter, opened a different cabinet, and chose a glass for me, a pretty glass with a stem, like for wine. She turned on the tap and held her finger under the water. After a minute, she filled the glass and handed it to me.

I took the Tylenols out of the bag in my pocket, popped them in my mouth, threw my head back, and tried to swallow the pills without gagging. When I opened my eyes, Morgan was reaching out for the glass. I handed it to her. She drank from it, then gave the glass back to me with just a little water left.

In my family we don't share glasses because of germs.

I closed my eyes and tipped the remains of the water into my mouth. Then I opened my eyes and looked her straight in the face. "I like Lou," I said.

"That again?" she pushed my shoulder.

I didn't budge. "Seriously."

"You do?" Morgan opened her eyes wide. "Lou Hochstetter?"

I nodded.

"Wow," Morgan said. "Lou. Really?"

"I know you think he's a geek," I said. "But I like him."

"I didn't think you liked anybody."

I shrugged.

Morgan lifted the glass out of my hand and refilled it. "Lou?"

"I know he's awkward, but don't you think . . . I don't know. My mother says sometimes the charming guys are the real losers."

"She's right," Morgan agreed, drinking the water. "My dad is charming, and he's the biggest bowel movement in the world."

I didn't know what to say to that.

She jumped off the counter. "Maybe your mother is right. Maybe I should like a geek, too."

"OK," I said, following her into her room.

"Maybe Gideon Weld," she said. "He's sort of a klutz."

"Yeah," I agreed.

"And he's friends with Lou, which would be fun. We could be, like, a foursome." We sat on the floor, our backs against her bed.

"That would be great." Then I whispered, "But what about Dex?"

"I didn't mean to tell you that." Morgan covered her face.

"I won't say anything."

"Good." She shook her head. "He'd never like me anyway. Gideon Weld, though. He wears brown socks in gym class. He'd have no right not to like somebody, right? OK. Here's what we have to do — we have to flirt."

"Maybe we should just ask them out."

"Please tell me you're kidding."

"Actually," I admitted, digging my fingers into her rug, "I already asked Lou out."

Morgan stared at me. "You did?"

I nodded. "Yeah. But he's not allowed to go out with anybody."

"So he said no? You asked him out and he said no? I would die!"

"Actually he said . . ."

"Wait, wait, wait. Tell me the whole thing, every single syllable." She grabbed her two pillows, handed me one, and hugged the other, all excited. "What did you say? Just 'Will you go out with me?'"

"Yeah." I felt a smile creeping onto my face, remembering.

"Where were you?" Morgan's eyes were open very wide. She chewed on the corner of her pillowcase.

"In Oakbrook Playground," I said. "On the swings."

Morgan grabbed me by the arms. "No way!" She gasped.

"Wait. It gets worse. He doesn't have great hearing, so he thought I was asking if he wanted a *garoudabee*."

"A what?"

"That's what he thought I said, 'Do you want a *garoudabee*?' Which isn't even a thing."

Morgan pushed me away and shouted, "No!"

I started to laugh. "I know. It was pretty tense for a minute there. I had to say it again."

"Again? What do you mean, again? You asked him out — twice?"

"Well . . ." I buried my head in the pillow. "Just because of his hearing."

"This is, I think, the funniest thing I ever heard. His hearing? I can't believe you didn't tell me!"

"I just did." I looked up at her. Her mouth was way open. I smiled.

Morgan closed her mouth. "When Tommy asked out CJ, she called me right away."

"I'm not CJ."

"True."

I punched the pillow down in my lap. "I've always thought it's so stupid that girls feel like they have to report all the intimate details of their lives to one another."

"Fine," Morgan said. "Don't. Not that I care." She stood up and threw her pillow back on her bed.

"No, wait. I meant, I always used to think that; it always seemed like such a, I don't know, an invasive requirement."

"Invasive?" She turned her back to me and fiddled with an eraser on her desk.

"Don't make fun of my vocabulary, Morgan. Please. I'm trying to tell you something. OK?"

She put the eraser down. "OK."

"That's what I always used to think — that it didn't make sense, confiding in somebody about private things." I got off the floor and sat down on her bed, still hugging the pillow. "But this is fun, telling you."

She came over and sat down next to me on the bed.

"I'm not good at this," I said. "I never, I don't . . ."

"Tell me more," she whispered.

"It was totally terrifying," I admitted. "Asking him the second time. I almost threw up." I hid my face in the pillow again. The pillowcase was worn so smooth it felt velvety.

Morgan put her arm around me. "He really said no?"

"Oh, no." I explained. "He said he wasn't allowed, but that he does like me."

"Oh," Morgan said. "Well . . ."

"He does! He gave me a cartoon."

"A what?"

I pulled the cartoon from my pocket and showed her. She read it and smiled. "He's good."

Morgan handed it back to me. While I folded it, she stood up and went back to her desk. She opened a drawer, pulled out the brown paper bag, and lifted my ring out of it. I watched her.

She blew the hair away from her eyes and came back to the bed. I reached out my hand. She smiled and placed the ring in my palm. I slipped it onto my finger, where it fit perfectly, and whispered, "Thanks."

She shrugged. "It looks good on you. We have to funk them. Lou and Gideon."

"Excuse me?"

"Funk," she repeated. "With an N."

We flipped over and hid our faces in her comforter for a minute, giggling. "What does that mean?" I finally asked.

"You never funked anybody?"

I shook my head. "I'm a virgin."

She hit me with the pillow, and said, "You pervert! It means you call your crush and then hang up when he answers!"

"Why in the world would you do that?"

"Trust me," she said. "Once you do it, you'll understand."

"Yeah?"

"You want me to go first?"

I nodded. We tiptoed out of her room and found the phone book in the front hall closet. We raced back into her room and together looked up Gideon Weld's number. "Here!"

She dialed, waited wide-eyed, then slammed down the phone. "Phew! Your turn."

"I know his number."

"I figured."

I dialed Lou's number. At the first ring, my palms started to sweat. I sat down cross-legged on her bed and closed my eyes. Second ring. I could barely catch my breath. I opened my eyes. Morgan was nodding.

"See?" she whispered.

"Hello?" Lou's voice in my ear.

I opened my mouth.

"Hang up!" Morgan mouthed. I gasped, looked at the phone, found the TALK button, and pressed it quick. Then I screeched and fell over backward on the bed, pulling Morgan's pillow over my face.

"See?" Morgan asked again, jumping on me.

I screeched again, and then the phone rang. I was under the pillow with me so it sounded like a fire alarm, it was so loud. Morgan and I both screamed. It rang again. "You answer," Morgan breathed, through her fingers.

I picked it up, pressed TALK, and said, "Hello?"

"Hello?" It was Lou.

"Lou?"

Morgan's mouth dropped open so wide I could see her tonsils.

"Olivia?" Lou asked.

"Yes," I squeaked. Morgan grabbed the pillow from me and crumpled it in her lap.

"Did you just call me?" Lou asked.

"Um," I said. "Yes. How did you know?"

"I did automatic callback," Lou said. "What happened?"

I covered the mouthpiece and whispered, "Star 69!"

Morgan opened her mouth wide, then screamed into the pillow.

"Olivia?" Lou asked.

"Um . . ." I grabbed the pillow from Morgan and screamed into it myself. Then I shook my head and, as calmly as possible, lifted the phone to my mouth again and said, "What?"

That cracked Morgan up. She grabbed the pillow back and laughed into it, rocking and repeating, "Star 69!"

Meanwhile, Lou was asking me, "Did you have an idea about our code?"

I tried to stifle my giggles. "Yeah," I lied, gasping for air and self-control. "Yeah, that's it. The math project!" The last two words came out sort of a scream. That was it; I lost it. I fell off the bed, laughing, listening to Lou asking, "Olivia? You OK?"

Morgan thumped her head against the mattress, giggling hysterically.

"Uh-huh," I managed.

"Well," Lou asked, "Do you want to go over it?"

"Now?" I screeched. "The math homework?" Morgan was rolling around on her bed, clutching herself.

"True, it's not due till Tuesday, but, do you want to sit together on the bus to apple picking? We could, like, work on it."

"I'm sitting with Morgan," I explained, looking at Morgan.

"Oh," Lou said.

Morgan jumped off the bed and grabbed me by the legs. "Say you have to go!" she whispered.

"I have to go," I told him.

"All right," Lou said.

"Thanks for calling," I said. "Back."

Morgan slapped her hands over her face.

"You're welcome," said Lou.

I hung up and screamed with Morgan. "I can't believe I did that. I made a total fool of myself!"

"Yes," Morgan agreed, nodding vigorously. "You sure did!"

"Aaa!" I screamed. I fell backward onto her bed, pulled my feet up, and laughed.

"Morgan!" her mother yelled.

We got serious fast. Morgan put her finger to her lips.

"Morgan!"

She lay silent beside me and held her hand up, above our heads. "These rings are nicer than I thought," she whispered.

I held mine up, next to hers. "They are nice," I agreed.

"I asked you for ten minutes of peace!" her mother screeched.

"Sorry," Morgan yelled.

"Can't you go outside?" her mother pleaded.

"Going," she answered without budging.

"Let's go for a bike ride," I suggested.

Still staring at our hands, she whispered to me, "What a couple of losers we are, huh?"

"I think we're great," I whispered.

"You would."

I shrugged.

Morgan knocked my hand lightly with hers. "So do I."

nineteen

I wrapped my arms around Morgan's waist as she started pedaling. She pumped really hard, and I closed my eyes to force myself not to steer. We banked around a corner. I just held onto her and tried to imagine us cemented together. It was very frightening, but at the same time, a little exciting.

I felt us picking up speed and had to open my eyes. We were heading down the steep hill on Oakbrook. I brake when I go down that hill all alone. I squeezed my eyes closed tight.

"Whew!" Morgan yelled as we picked up more speed.

I told myself to sit still and hold on. *Don't lean!* Stop imagining the hospital emergency room and my father racing in, in his surgical scrubs with his beeper lighting up, furious and disappointed in my judgment.

Trust her.

The road flattened out. I opened my eyes and loosened my grip. Slightly.

"That was great!" Morgan yelled, pedaling again.

"Yeah," I agreed. "It was."

"We did it!"

"Whew!" I yelled. We bobbled a little. I gripped her tighter. We didn't fall. I sat up straighter and reminded myself to breathe. After two or three breaths, I had relaxed enough to let myself look around. We were passing Oakbrook Playground, where I used to play.

Check out this sneak preview from

popularity contest

When I got to school Monday morning, it was drizzling. Morgan and CJ were sitting up on the wall together, with the hoods of their windbreakers up. Morgan was whispering in CJ's ear and CJ was nodding. I waved at them and smiled. CJ looked down, Morgan looked away.

I didn't stop smiling. I started to climb up to sit on the wall with them, but the warning bell rang and they jumped down. None of us gets free breakfast, so we usually just wait for the second bell.

"Hey, guys," I said. I had forgotten my rain jacket, so I gathered my hair and twisted it, hoping to avoid frizz.

"Hi," CJ said, quietly, without making eye contact.

"Tommy and Jonas had lots of posters with them," I told them. "On the bus this morning. For Lou. For class president."

"If you wanted . . ." CJ straightened her legs so tight, they looked curved backwards. "We, if you want posters, we . . ."

"No," I assured her. "I don't really care. Boy, it's really starting to rain."

Olivia wandered over to us, her umbrella up to shield her and the paperback book she was reading. She stood in front of us like that for a few seconds.

Morgan, CJ, and I all waited, shrugging at each other. When Olivia lowered the book, she blinked a few times. She looked surprised to find herself in front of us, at school.

"It's raining," she mentioned.

The second bell rang and the four of us, our little clique, walked into school without talking. On the way we passed my cousin Gabriela hanging a poster on the lobby bulletin board. It was on red oak tag and it said, in blue marker, LOU is WHO will DO. There were gobs of glitter in pools of dried white glue.

I didn't want to be the one to comment.

At the lockers, we all dialed our combinations (except Olivia, who bent to use her key) and dumped our extra stuff in. There was a big clattering of the hollow metal being pounded by old, heavy texts. CJ, Morgan, and Olivia wiggled out of their wet windbreakers. I shook myself off, slammed my locker shut and waited; I don't like to be slow.

"Well, it rhymes," Olivia said, closing her locker gently. "But I guess Lou is an easy name to rhyme."

"Oh," CJ said. "Here." She handed me Big Blue, my favorite sweatshirt. I had given it to her the day we became best friends, after she rode her bike over to my house to tell me Tommy had asked her out. She had been sitting on my bed shivering, so I'd given her Big

Blue, my most special thing in the world, and I'd felt good about it, like I had grown up, like — see, she is more important to me than anything, than any *thing*.

I didn't stretch out my hand to take it. I hadn't said I wanted it back.

"I washed it," CJ said, as if I were afraid it was dirty.

I took it and while I redialed my combination, I smelled Big Blue. It didn't smell like Big Blue anymore. I placed it gently on the top shelf of my locker, closed the door, and jiggled the lock. Then I remembered to say, "Thanks."

I noticed I was twirling a piece of my hair, a habit I'd broken — and gotten a Minnie Mouse Pez dispenser for breaking — when I was five years old. I forced my hand into my tight jeans pocket. Not that my mother would remember and take the Pez dispenser away now, as she had warned she'd do if I went back to twirling, but on principle.

Olivia pushed her lower lip away from her braces and said to me, "I'm sure your posters will be good, too."

"I don't care," I mumbled.

"Ew," screeched Morgan. "What's that?" She was pointing at the floor, where there was a liquid trail of red.

We all gasped, with the same thought in our heads:

Is somebody bleeding? I quickly looked down at my jeans, and tried to be casual about looking at my behind — all the while praying, *please let it not be me.*

"Is it me?" Morgan asked nervously. She showed her behind. We all shook our heads.

"It can't be me," Olivia said, checking her pants to be sure, anyway. "I doubt I'll get my period before I'm sixteen."

I swallowed hard. I didn't get mine in July or August, but Devin promised me that's pretty common when you're just starting. "Is it me?" I asked nervously. I didn't feel anything, inside me, but I've only had my period five times so I'm not such an expert at all on the way it feels.

My friends looked me over.

CJ gasped.

"Oh, no," I moaned.

Rachel Vail has written four other well-received novels for adolescents, including WONDER, an *American Bookseller* "Pick of the Lists," which Judy Blume called "Wonderful!"; DARING TO BE ABIGAIL, a *School Library Journal* Best Book of the Year; DO–OVER, a Recommended Book for Reluctant Young Readers; and EVER AFTER, which was one of the New York Public Library's 100 Best Children's Books in 1994.

She lives with her husband and young son in New York City.